John Habberton

Country Luck

John Habberton

Country Luck

ISBN/EAN: 9783337227975

Printed in Europe, USA, Canada, Australia, Japan

Cover: Foto ©Andreas Hilbeck / pixelio.de

More available books at **www.hansebooks.com**

BY
JOHN HABBERTON,
AUTHOR OF

"BRUETON'S BAYOU," ETC.

PHILADELPHIA:

J. B. LIPPINCOTT COMPANY.

1887.

CONTENTS.

COUNTRY LUCK.

CHAPTER I.

HOW IT CAME ABOUT.

"BE sure to look us up when you come to the city."

This invitation was extended with that delightful affectation of heartiness that a man can assume when he believes that the person invited will never avail himself of the courtesy. Fortunately for the purpose of this story, Master Philip Hayn, whom Mr. Tramlay had asked to call, was too young and too unaccustomed to the usages of polite society to regard the remark in any but its actual sense.

It would have seemed odd to any one knowing the two men and their respective stations in life. Tramlay was a New York merchant, well known and of fair standing in the iron trade; Hayn was son of the farmer at whose house the Tramlay family had passed the summer. When the Tramlays determined to exchange the late summer dust of the country for the early autumn dust of the city, it was Philip who drove the old-fashioned carryall that transported them from the farm to the railway-station. The head of the merchant's family was attired like a well-to-do business-man; Philip's coat, vest, and trousers were remnants of three different suits, none of recent cut. The contrast was made sharper by the easy condescension of the older man and the rather awkward deference of Philip, and it moved Mrs. Tramlay to whisper, as her husband helped her aboard the train,—

"Suppose he were to take you at your word, Edgar?"

The merchant shrugged his shoulders slightly, and replied, "Worse men have called upon us, my dear, without being made to feel unwelcome."

"I think 'twould be loads of fun," remarked Miss Lucia Tramlay.

Then the three, followed by smaller members of the family, occupied as many seats near windows, and nodded smiling adieus as the train started.

Philip returned their salutations, except the smiles: somehow, the departure of all these people made him feel sober. He followed the train with his eyes until it was out of sight; then he stepped into the old carryall and drove briskly homeward, declining to rein up and converse with the several sidewalk-loungers who manifested a willingness to converse about the departed guests. When he reached the outer edge of the little village he allowed the horses to relapse into their normal gait, which was a slow walk; he let the reins hang loosely, he leaned forward until his elbows rested upon his knees and his hat-brim seemed inclined to scrape acquaintance with the dash-board, then he slowly repeated,—

"'Be sure to look us up when you come to the city.' You may be sure that I will."

The advent of the Tramlays at Hayn Farm had
been productive of new sensations to all concerned.
The younger members of the Tramlay family had at
first opposed the plan of a summer on a farm: they
had spent one season at Mount Desert, and part of
another at Saratoga, and, as Lucia had been "out"
a year, and had a sister who expected early admission to a metropolitan collection of rosebuds, against
a summer in the country—the rude, common, real
country—the protests had been earnest. But the
head of the family had said he could not afford anything better; trade was dull, a man had to live
within his income, etc. Besides, their mother's
health was not equal to a summer in society: they
would find that statement a convenient excuse when
explaining the family plans to their friends.

Arrived at Hayn Farm, the objections of the juve-
nile Tramlays quickly disappeared. Everything
was new and strange; nothing was repellent, and
much was interesting and amusing: what more
could they have hoped for anywhere,—even in
Paris? The farm was good and well managed, the
rooms neat and comfortable though old-fashioned,
and the people intelligent, though Miss Lucia pronounced them "awfully funny." The head of the
family was one of the many farmers who "took
boarders" to give his own family an opportunity to
see people somewhat unlike their own circle of acquaintances,—an opportunity which they seemed un-
likely ever to find in any other way, had he been able
to choose. The senior Hayn would have put into
his spare rooms a Union Theological Seminary pro-

fessor with his family, but, as no such person responded to his modest advertisement, he accepted an iron-merchant and family instead.

Strawberries were just ripening when the Tramlays appeared at Hayn Farm, and the little Tramlays were allowed to forage at will on the capacious old strawberry-bed; then came other berries, in the brambles of which they tore their clothes and colored their lips for hours at a time. Then cherries reddened on a dozen old trees which the children were never reminded had not been planted for their especial benefit. Then the successive yield of an orchard was theirs, so far as they could absorb it. Besides, there was a boat on a pond, and another on a little stream that emptied into the ocean not far away; and although the Hayn boys always seemed to have work to do, they frequently could be persuaded to accompany the children to keep them from drowning themselves.

For Mrs. Tramlay, who really was an invalid, there were long drives to be taken, over roads some of which were well shaded and others commanding fine views, and it was so restful to be able to drive without special preparation in the way of dress,— without, too, the necessity of scrutinizing each approaching vehicle for fear it might contain some acquaintance who ought to be recognized.

As for the head of the family, who spent only Saturdays and Sundays with his family, he seemed to find congenial society in the head of the house,— a fact which at first gave his wife great uneasiness and annoyance.

"Edgar," Mrs. Tramlay would say, "you know Mr. Hayn is only a common farmer."

"He's respectable, and thoroughly understands his own business," the husband replied,—"two reasons, either of which is good enough to make me like a man, unless he happens to be disagreeable. 'Common farmer'! Why, I'm only a common iron-merchant, my dear."

"That's different," protested Mrs. Tramlay.

"Is it? Well, don't try to explain how, little woman: 'twill be sure to give you a three days' headache."

So Tramlay continued to devote hours to chat with his host, pressing high-priced cigars on him, and sharing the farmer's pipes and tobacco in return. He found that Hayn, like any other farmer with brains, had done some hard thinking in the thousands of days when his hands were employed at common work, and that his views of affairs in general, outside of the iron trade, were at least as sound as Tramlay's own, or those of any one whom Tramlay knew in the city.

The one irreconcilable member of the family was the elder daughter, Lucia. She was the oldest child, so she had her own way; she was pretty, so she had always been petted; she was twenty, so she knew everything that she thought worth knowing. She had long before reconstructed the world (in her own mind) just as it should be, from the stand-point that it ought to exist solely for her benefit. Not bad-tempered, on the contrary, cheerful and full of high spirits, she was nevertheless in perpetual protest

against everything that was not exactly as she would
have it, and not all the manners that careful breeding could impart could restrain the unconscious in-
solence peculiar to young and self-satisfied natures.
She would laugh loudly at table at Mrs. Hayn's way
of serving an omelet, tell Mrs. Hayn's husband that
his Sunday coat looked "so funny," express her
mind freely, before the whole household, at the horrid
way in which the half-grown Hayn boys wore their
hair, and had no hesitation in telling Philip Hayn,
two years her senior, that when he came in from the
field in his brown flannel shirt and gray felt hat he
looked like an utter guy. But the Hayns were human,
and, between pity and admiration, humanity long
ago resolved to endure anything from a girl—if she
is pretty.

Slowly the Hayns came to like their boarders ;
more slowly, but just as surely, the Tramlays learned
to like their hosts. Mutual respect began at the
extremes of both families. Mrs. Tramlay, being a
mother and a housekeeper, became so interested in the
feminine half of the family's head that she ceased to
criticise her husband's interest in the old farmer.
The Tramlay children wondered at, and then admired, the wisdom and skill of their country companions in matters not understood by city children.
Last of all, Lucia found herself heartily respecting
the farmer's son, and forgetting his uncouth dress
and his awkwardness of manner in her wonder at
his general courtesy, and his superior knowledge in
some directions where she supposed she had gone as
far as possible. She had gone through a finishing-

school of the most approved New York type, yet
Philip knew more of languages and history and
science than she, when they chanced—never through
her fault—to converse on such dry subjects; he knew
more flowers than she had ever seen in a florist's shop
in the city; and once when she had attempted to
decorate the rather bare walls of the farm-house
parlor he corrected her taste with a skill which she
was obliged to admit. There was nothing strange
about it, except to Lucia; for city seminaries and
country high schools use the same text-books, and
magazines and newspapers that give attention to
home decorations go everywhere; nevertheless, it
seemed to Lucia that she had discovered a new order
of being, and by the time she had been at Hayn Farm
a month she found herself occasionally surprised
into treating Philip almost as if he were a gentleman.

Philip's interest in Lucia was of much quicker
development. He had had no prejudices to overcome; besides, the eye is more easily approached and
satisfied than the intellect, and Lucia had acceptably
filled many an eye more exacting than the young
farmer's. There were pretty girls in homes near
Hayn Farm, and more in the village near by, but
none of them were——well, none were exactly like
Lucia. Philip studied her face; it was neither Roman
nor Grecian, and he was obliged to confess that the
proportions of her features were not so good as those
of some girls in the neighborhood. Her figure suggested neither perfect grace nor perfect strength;
and yet whatever she did was gracefully done, and
her attire, whether plain or costly, seemed part of

herself,—a peculiarity that he had never observed among girls born in the vicinity. He soon discovered that she did not know everything, but whatever she did know she talked of so glibly that he could not help enjoying the position of listener. She did not often show earnestness about anything that to him was more than trifling, but when she did go out of her customary mood for a moment or two she was saintly: he could think of no other word that would do it justice. He had not liked her manner to his own mother, for at first the girl treated that estimable woman as a servant, and did it in the manner which makes most servants detest most young ladies; but had she not afterward, with her own tiny fingers, made a new Sunday bonnet for Mrs. Hayn, and had not his mother, in genuine gratitude, kissed her? Should he bear malice for what his mother had forgiven?

The young man merely admired and respected Lucia: of that he was very sure. Regard more tender he would have blamed himself for, first, because love implied matrimony, which he did not intend to venture into until he had seen more of the world and perhaps gone to college; secondly, because he did not imagine that any such sentiment would be reciprocated. He came of a family that through generations of hard experience had learned to count the cost of everything, even the affections, like most of the better country-people in the older States. He had also an aversion to marriage between persons of different classes. Lucia was to him an acquaintance,—not even a friend,—whom he highly esteemed; that was all.

His father thought differently, and one day when the two were in the woodland belonging to the farm, loading a wagon with wood to be stored near the house for winter use, the old man said, abruptly,—

"I hope you're not growin' too fond of that young woman, Phil?"

"No danger," the youth answered, promptly, though as he raised his head his eyes did not meet his father's.

"You seem to know who I mean, anyhow," said the old man, after throwing another stick of wood upon the wagon.

"Not much trouble to do that," Phil replied. "There's only one young woman."

The father laughed softly; the son blushed violently. Then the father sighed.

"That's one of the signs."

"What's a sign?—sign of what?" said Phil, affecting wonder not quite skilfully.

"When 'there's only one young woman' it's a sign the young man who thinks so is likely to consider her the only one worth thinkin' about."

"Oh, pshaw!" exclaimed Phil, attacking the woodpile with great industry.

"Easy, old boy; 'twasn't the wood-pile that said it. Brace up your head; you've done nothing to be ashamed of. Besides, your old father can see through the back of your head, anyhow : he's been practisin' at it ever since you were born."

Phil seated himself on the wood-pile, looked in the direction where his father was not, and said,—

"I like Lucia very much. She's a new face; she's

2

different from the girls about here. She's somebody
new to talk to, and she can talk about something beside crops, and cows, and who is sick, and last Sunday's sermon, and next month's sewing-society.
That's all."

"Yes," said the old man. "It doesn't seem much,
does it? Enough to have made millions of bad
matches, though, and spoiled millions of good ones."

Phil was silent for a moment; then he said, with a
laugh,—

"Father, I believe you're as bad as old Mrs. Trip-
sey, whom mother's always laughing at because she
thinks a man's in love if he sees her daughter home
from prayer-meeting."

"P'r'aps so, my boy,—p'r'aps,—and maybe as bad
as you, for every time there's a bad thunder-storm
you're afraid the lightning'll strike the barn. Do
you know why? It's because your finest colt is
there. Do you see?"

Phil did not reply, so the old man continued:

"I'll make it clearer to you. You're my finest
colt; there's more lightnings in a girl's eyes than I
ever saw in the sky, you don't know when it's going
to strike, and when it hits you you're gone before you
know it."

"Much obliged. I'll see to it that I keep myself
well insulated," said Phil.

Nevertheless, Phil studied Lucia whenever he had
opportunity,—studied her face when she read, her
fingers when they busied themselves with fancy
work, her manner with different persons, as it
changed according to her idea of the deservings of

those with whom she talked. At church he regarded her intently from the beginning of the service to its end, analyzing such portions of prayer, hymn, or sermon as did not seem to meet her views. He even allowed his gaze to follow her when she looked more than an instant at other young women, in the ignorance of his masculine heart wondering which of the features of these damsels specially interested her; his mother could have told him that Lucia was merely looking at bonnets and other articles of attire, instead of at their wearers. He wondered what she thought; he told himself where her character was at fault, and how it might be improved. In short, he had ample mental leisure, and she was the newest and consequently the least understood of his various subjects of contemplation.

It is impossible to devote a great deal of thought to any subject without becoming deeply interested, even if it be unsightly, tiresome, and insignificant. Lucia was none of these, for she was a pretty girl. It is equally impossible to see a familiar subject of thought in the act of disappearance without a personal sense of impending loneliness, and a wild desire to snatch it back or at least go in search of it. Therefore Philip Hayn needed not to be in love, or even to think himself so, to be conscious of a great vacancy in his mind as the train bore the Tramlay family rapidly toward their city home, and to determine that he would avail himself of the invitation which the head of the family had extended.

CHAPTER II.

"HUSBAND," said Mrs. Hayn to her husband one night, when the person addressed was about to drop asleep, "something's the matter with Phil."

"A touch of malaria, I suppose," said the farmer. "He's been gettin' out muck earlier than usual, and spreadin' it on the ridge of the pasture. The sun's been pretty hot, though it is October, and hot sun on that sort of stuff always breeds malaria."

"I wasn't talkin' of sickness," said the wife. "The dear boy's health is as good as ever. It's his mind that's out o' sorts."

A long soft sigh was the farmer's only reply for a moment. It was followed by the remark,—

"That city gal, I s'pose,—confound her!"

"I don't see what you want her confounded for: she hasn't done anythin'. They don't correspond."

"I should hope not," said Hayn, with considerable vigor: he now was wide awake, "What could they write about? You don't s'pose Phil could write anythin' about our goin's-on that would interest her, do you?"

"No, but young people sometimes do find somethin' to exchange letters about. You and I didn't, when we were boy and girl, because we lived within

16

a stone's throw of each other, an' you couldn't keep away from our house after dark ; but Philip and——"

"For goodness sake, old lady," interrupted the husband, "don't you go to settin' yourself down, at your time of life, by gettin' the match-makin' fever. There isn't the slightest chance that——"

"I didn't say there was ; but boys will be boys."

"It doesn't follow that they should be fools, does it?—not when they're *our* boys ?"

"'Tisn't bein' a fool to be interested in a rich man's daughter. I've often thought how different your life might have been if I'd had anything besides myself to give you when you married me."

"I got all I expected, and a thousand times more than I deserved." This assertion was followed by a kiss, which, though delivered in the dark, was of absolutely accurate aim.

"Don't put it into Phil's head that he can get more than a wife when he marries ; 'twill do him a great deal more harm than good."

"I'd like to see the dear boy so fixed that he won't have to work so hard as you've had to do."

"Then you'll see him less of a man than his father, when he ought to be better. Isn't that rather poor business for a mother in Israel to be in, old lady?"

"Well, anyhow, I believe Phil's heart is set on makin' a trip down to York."

"Oh, is that all? Well, he's been promised it, for some day, this long while. Something's always prevented it, but I s'pose now would be as good a time as any. He deserves it; he's as good a son as man ever had."

b　　　　　2*

Mrs. Hayn probably agreed with her husband as
to the goodness of their son, but that was not the
view of him in which she was interested just then.
Said she,—

"If he goes, of course he'll see *her.*"

Again the farmer sighed; then he said, quite earnestly,—

"Let him see her, then; the sooner he does it the
sooner he'll stop thinkin' about her. Bless your dear
foolish old heart, her ways and his are as far apart as
Haynton and heaven when there's a spiritual drought
in this portion of the Lord's vineyard."

"*I* don't think the Tramlays are so much better
than we, if they *have* got money," said Mrs. Hayn,
with some indignation. "I always did say that you
didn't set enough store by yourself. Mrs. Tramlay
is a nice enough woman, but I never could see how
she was any smarter than I; and as to her husband,
I always noticed that you generally held your own
when the two of you were talking about anything."

"Bless you!" exclaimed the farmer, "you *are*
rather proud of your old husband, aren't you? But
Phil will soon see, with half an eye, that it would be
the silliest thing in the world for him to fall in love
with a girl like that."

"I can't for the life of me see why," said the
mother. "He's just as good as she, and a good deal
smarter, or I'm no judge."

"See here, Lou Ann," said the farmer, with more
than a hint of impatience in his voice, "you know
'twon't do either of 'em any good to fall in love if
they can't marry each other. An' what would Phil

have to support his wife on? Would she come out here an' 'tend to all the house-work of the farm, like you do, just for the sake of havin' Phil for a husband? Not unless she's a fool, even if Phil *is* our boy an' about as good as they make 'em. An' you know well enough that he couldn't afford to live in New York: he's got nothin' to do it on."

"Not now, but he might go in business there, and make enough to live in style. Other young fellows have done it!"

"Yes,—in stories," said the old man. "Lou Ann, don't you kind o' think that for a church-member of thirty years' standin' you're gettin' mighty worldly-minded?"

"No, I don't," Mrs. Hayn answered. "If not to want my boy to drudge away his life like his father's done is bein' worldly, then I'm goin' to be a backslider, an' stay one. I don't think 'twould be a bit bad to have a married son down to York, so's his old mother could have some place to go once in a while when she's tired to death of work an' worry."

"Oho!" said the old man: "that's the point of it, eh? Well, I don't mind backslidin' enough myself to say the boy may marry one of Satan's daughters, if it'll make life any easier for you, old lady."

"Much obliged," the mother replied, "but I don't know as I care to do visitin' down there."

The conversation soon subsided, husband and wife dropping into revery from which they dropped into slumber. In one way or other, however, the subject came up again. Said Mrs. Hayn one day, just as her husband was leaving the dinner-table for the field in which he was cutting and stacking corn,—

"I do believe Phil's best coat is finer stuff than anything Mr. Tramlay wore when they were up here. I don't believe what he wore Sundays could hold a candle to Phil's."

"Like enough," said the farmer; "and yet the old man always looked better dressed. I think his clothes made him look a little younger than Phil, too."

"Now, husband, you know it isn't fair to make fun of the dear boy's clothes in that way. You know well enough that the stuff for his coat was cut from the same bolt of broadcloth as the minister's best."

"Yes," drawled the farmer through half a dozen inflections, any one of which would have driven frantic any woman but his own wife.

"It's real mean in you to say 'Yes' in that way, Reuben !"

"'Tisn't the wearer that makes the man, old lady; it's the tailor."

"I'm sure Sarah Tweege cut an' made Phil's coat, an' if there's a better sewin'-woman in this part of the county I'd like to know where you find her."

"Oh, Sarah Tweege can sew, Lou Ann," the old man admitted. "Goodness ! I wish she'd made my new harness, instead of whatever fellow did it. Mebbe, too, if she'd made the sacks for the last oats I bought I wouldn't have lost about half a bushel on the way home. Yesm', Sarah Tweege can sew a bed-quilt up as square as an honest man's conscience. But sewin' ain't tailorin'."

"Don't she always make the minister's clothes?" demanded Mrs. Hayn.

"I never thought of it before, but of course she does. I don't believe anybody else could do it in that way. Yet the minister ain't got so bad a figure, when you see him workin' in his garden, in his shirt-sleeves."

"It's time for you to go back to the cornfield," suggested Mrs. Hayn.

"Yes, I reckon 'tis," said the farmer, caressing what might have been nap had not his old hat been of felt. "'Tain't safe for an old farmer to be givin' his time an' thought to pomps an' vanities,—like the minister's broadcloth coat."

"Get out !" exclaimed Mrs. Hayn, with a threatening gesture. The old man kissed her, laughed, and began to obey her command ; but as, like countrymen in general, he made his exit by the longest possible route, wandering through the sitting-room, the hall, the dining-room, and the kitchen, his wife had time to waylay him at the door-step and remark,—

"I was only goin' to say that if Phil does make that trip to York I don't see that he'll need to buy new clothes. He's never wore that Sunday coat on other days, except to two or three funerals an' parties. I was goin' it over this very mornin', an' it's about as good as new."

"I wonder how this family would ever have got along if I hadn't got such a caretakin' wife?" said the old man. "It's the best coat in the United States, if *you've* been goin' it over."

Phil was already in the corn,—he had left the table

some minutes before his father,—and as the old man approached, Phil said,—

"Father, don't you think that wind-break for the sheep needs patching this fall?"

"It generally does, my son, before cold weather sets in."

"I guess I'll get at it, then, as soon as we get the corn stacked."

"What's the hurry? The middle of November is early enough for that."

"Oh, when it's done it'll be off our minds."

"See here, old boy," said the father, dropping the old ship's cutlass with which he had begun to cut the corn-stalks, "you're doin' all your work a month ahead this fall. What are you goin' to do with all your time when there's no more work to be done?"

"I can't say, I'm sure," said Phil, piling an armful of stalks against a stack with more than ordinary care.

"Can't, eh? Then I'll have to, I s'pose, seein' I'm your father. I guess I'll have to send you down to New York for a month, to look aroun' an' see somethin' of the world."

Phil turned so quickly that he ruined all his elaborate work of the moment before, almost burying his father under the toppling stack.

"That went to the spot, didn't it?" said the old man. "I mean the proposition,—not the fodder," he continued, as he extricated himself from the mass of corn-stalks.

"It's exactly what I've been wanting to do," said Phil, "but——"

"But you didn't like to say so, eh? Well, 'twasn't necessary to mention it; as I told you t'other day, I can see through the back of your head any time, old boy."

"'Twouldn't cost much money," said Phil. "I could go down on Sol Mantring's sloop for nothing, some time when he's short-handed."

"Guess I can afford to pay my oldest son's travellin' expenses when I send him out to see the world. You'll go down to York by railroad, an' in the best car, too, if there's any difference."

"I won't have to buy clothes, anyhow," said the younger man.

"Yes, you will,—lots of 'em. York ain't Haynton, old boy; an' as the Yorkers don't know enough to take their style from you, you'll have to take yours from them. I was there once, when I was 'long about your age: I didn't have to buy no more meetin'-clothes after that until I got married,—nigh on to ten years."

"If it's as expensive as that, I'm not going," said Phil, looking very solemn and beginning to reconstruct the demolished stack.

"Yes, you are, sir. I'll have you understand you're not much over age yet, an' have got to mind your old father. Now let that corn alone. If it won't stay down, sit on it,—this way,—see." And, suiting the action to the word, the old man sprawled at ease on the fallen fodder, dragged his son down after him, and said,—

"You shall have a hundred dollars to start with, and more afterward, if you need it, as I know you will. The first thing to do when you get to the city is to go to the best-looking clothing-store you can find, and buy a suit such as you see well-dressed men wearing to business. Keep your eyes open on men as sharply as if they were hosses and clothes were their only points, and then see that you get as good clothes as any of them. It don't matter so much about the stuff; but have your clothes fit you, an' cut like other people's."

"I don't want to put on city airs," said Phil.

"That's right,—that's right; but city clothes and city airs aren't any more alike than country airs an' good manners. You may be the smartest, brightest young fellow that ever went to York,—as of course you are, bein' my son,—but folks at York'll never find it out if you don't dress properly,—that means, dress as they do. I'll trade watches with you, to trade back after the trip: mine is gold, you know. You'll have to buy a decent chain, though."

"I won't take your watch, father. I can't; that's all about it."

"Nonsense! of course you can, if you try. It isn't good manners to wear silver watches in the city."

"But your watch——" Phil could get no further; for his father's gold watch was venerated by the family as if it were a Mayflower chair or the musket of a soldier of the Revolution. Once while old farmer Hayn was young Captain Hayn, of the whaling-ship Lou Ann, he saved the crew of a sinking British bark. Unlike modern ship-captains (who do not own their vessels), he went in the boat with the rescuing-party instead of merely sending it out, and he suffered so much through exposure, strain, and the fear of the death which seemed impending that he abandoned the sea as soon thereafter as possible. Nevertheless he thought only of the work before him, until he had rescued the imperilled crew and stowed them safely in his own ship. The circumstances of the rescue were so unusual that they formed the subject of long columns in foreign newspapers; and in a few months Captain Hayn received through the State Department at Washington a gold watch, with sundry complimentary papers from the British Admiralty. The young seaman never talked of either; his neighbors first learned of the presentation by conning their favorite weekly newspapers; nevertheless the papers were framed and hung in the young captain's bedchamber, and, however carelessly he dressed afterward, nobody ever saw him when he had not the watch in his pocket.

"Father," said Phil, after some moments spent in silence and facial contortion, "I can't take your watch, even for a little while. You've always worn it: it's your—the family's—patent of nobility."

"Well," said the old farmer, after contemplating the toes of his boots a few seconds, "I don't mind ownin' up to my oldest son that I look at the old watch in about the same light; but a patent of nobility is a disgrace to a family if the owner's heir isn't fit to inherit it. See? Guess you'd better make up your mind to break yourself into your comin' responsibilities, by carryin' that watch in New York. Wonder what time 'tis?"

The question was a good pretext on which to take

the ".patent of nobility" from his fob-pocket and
look at it. He did it in a way which caused Phil
quickly to avert his face and devote himself with
great industry to stacking corn. Half a minute later
the old man, cutlass in hand, was cutting corn as if
his life depended upon it.

CHAPTER III.

"DOWN TO YORK."

DESPITE his father's expressed desire, Phil went to New York on Sol Mantring's sloop. The difference in time promised to be a day or two days, but the difference in cash outlay was more than five dollars,— a sum which no one in the vicinity of Hayn Farm had ever been known to spend needlessly without coming to grief. Between cash in hand and its nominal equivalent in time, Phil, like most other prudent young countrymen, had learned to distinguish with alacrity and positiveness: besides, he knew how small was the amount of ready money that his father, in spite of care and skill at his business, was able to show for more than a quarter of a century of hard work.

The young man's departure was the occasion for quite a demonstration by the neighbors. Other young men of the vicinage had been to New York, but generally they were those whom their neighbors did not hope to see again; Phil, on the contrary, was a general favorite. His family intended that no one should know of the journey until Phil was fairly off, for they knew by experience, in which sometimes they had been the offenders, how insatiable is rural curiosity about any doings out of the ordinary. But

27

when Sol Mantring told his wife that Phil was to go
down with him as a "hand," Mrs. Mantring straight-
way put on her best things and went out to tell all
her neighbors that Phil Hayn was going down to
York, and, being a woman who never did anything
by halves, she afterward plodded the dusty road that
led to the little village at the railway-station, where
she consumed several hours in doing petty shopping
at the several stores, varying this recreation by indus-
trious gossip with every acquaintance who dropped
in. As each person who heard the news wondered
what Phil was going for, and as Mrs. Mantring was
sure she didn't know any better than dead-and-gone
Adam, there was developed a wealth of surmise and
theory that should have forever dispelled the general
impression that Americans are not an imaginative
people.

For the remainder of Phil's time at home the family
and its eldest son had scarcely enough time to themselves to attend. to their daily devotions. People
came to borrow something, to bring news, to ask
advice,—anything that would be an excuse to see
what might be going on and to learn why Phil was
going to the city. Phil's parents had prepared what
they supposed would be sufficient explanation : the
farm and the house needed some things that could
better be selected from large stocks and variety than
bought nearer home. But they had underrated the
persistency of local curiosity : numberless pointed
questions were asked, and if in the course of a week
there had been any visitor who did not ask, in one
way or other, whether Phil would go to see the

Tramlays, the family did not know who it had been; they were sure they would have gratefully noted such a considerate person at the time, and remembered him—or her—forever after.

There were scores, too, who wanted Phil to do them small services in the city. Farmer Blewitt had heard that the car-companies often sold for almost nothing the horses that broke down at their hard work and needed only plenty of rest and pasturage to make them as good as new : wouldn't Phil look about and see if he couldn't get him a bargain ?—and bring it back on the sloop, if he wouldn't mind feeding and watering it on the home trip ! Old Mrs. Wholley had been finding her spectacles so young that she didn't know but she needed stronger glasses, or maybe a Bible with larger print: if Phil would price both and write her, she would try to make up her mind what she ought to do. Samantha Roobles had been telling her husband James for the last five years that their best-room carpet was too shabby for people who might have a funeral in the family at any time, James's stepmother being very old and sickly, but James wouldn't do anything but put off, and as for her, she wasn't going to be cheated out of her eye-teeth at the stores at the dépôt, when year before last she saw in a York newspaper, that the wind blew out of the hand of somebody leaning out of a train window, that good ingrains were selling in New York at thirty-five cents a yard : she wished Phil would pick her out one.

Besides many requests like these, Phil had to make promises to dozens of young men and women whose

3*

wants were smaller, but none the easier to attend to :
so the prospective traveller and his parents had the
pains of parting alleviated by the thought that not
until Phil departed would any of them have peace.
The day of sailing brought a great throng of visitors,—so many that the minister, who was of the number, extemporized a "neighborhood prayer-meeting,"
at which Providence was implored to "save our dear
young brother from the perils of the deep," and informed of so many of Phil's good qualities that only
an inborn respect for religious forms restrained the
modest youth from sneaking out of the back door
and hiding in the hull of the sloop until there was a
broad expanse of water between him and the shore.

Then the entire throng, excepting two or three old
ladies who remained with Mrs. Hayn "to help her
bear up, poor soul," escorted Phil to the sloop. Among
them was a predominance of young men who looked
as if in case Phil should want a substitute they were
ready, and of young women whose faces indicated
that if Phil should care to say anything tender to
anybody, just to have something to think about while
away, he should have no excuse to leave it unsaid.
Sol Mantring cut the parting short by remarking
that prayer was all very well in its place, but he didn't
believe in it keeping a sloop in a shallow river while
the tide was falling and no wind to help her out. So
Phil hurried aboard, though not before his father had
almost crushed his hand with a grasp that had been
developed by many years of training with bridle-
reins, axe-helves, and paternal affection.

Some one cast off the sloop's hawser ; the mainsail

was already up, and the craft began to drift out with the tide. This was the signal for a flutter of handkerchiefs and a chorus of cheers, during which Farmer Hayn plodded along the river-bank beside the sloop, regardless of mud, stones, marsh grass and cat-tails. He seemed to have no last injunctions for his boy ; indeed, his occasional shouts were bestowed principally upon Sol Mantring, who stood at the wheel, and they had no more relation to Phil than to the Khan of Khiva. In like manner Phil seemed less interested in his father than in the maze of cordage at the foot of the mast. Nevertheless, when the river-bank ended at the shore of the bay, and could be followed no longer, the old man stood there, as Sol Mantring said afterward, "lookin' as if he'd lost his last friend, never expected to git another, an' he'd got ten year older all of a sudden," and Phil, when he saw this, straightened in front of the friendly mast which hid him from the remainder of the crew, and threw kisses to his father, with the profusion of early childhood, as long as he could distinguish the dingy old coat and hat from the stones of similar hue that marked the little point.

"The perils of the deep" were happily averted. Indeed, Phil would willingly have endured more could the wind have blown harder. The sloop finally made her pier in New York about dusk of the second day. Phil hastily donned his best suit, and as the part of the city in which the iron-merchants cluster was not far away, and Sol Mantring knew the streets of that portion of the city, Phil started, with minute directions from the skipper, to call on Mr. Tramlay.

His singleness of purpose made him unconscious that he was acting in a manner not common to him, but as he climbed the side of the pier and hurried toward the mass of light before him Sol Mantring remarked to the remainder of the crew, consisting of two men,—

"I knowed it."

"Knowed what?"

"He's gal-struck. Got it bad."

Phil made his way up the principal thoroughfare from New York to Brooklyn, wondering at the thronged sidewalks and brilliantly-lighted shops, but he did not neglect to eye the street-names on corner-lamps. Soon he turned into a street which was part of his course as laid down by Sol; at the same time he turned from light to darkness, the change being almost appalling in its suddenness. Still he hurried on, and after another turn began to look for numbers on the fronts of buildings. His heart bounded within him as he suddenly saw, by the light of a street-lamp, the sign EDGAR TRAMLAY. In an instant his hand was on the door-knob; but the door did not open. Through the glass door he saw two or three dim lights within. Probably the proprietor was at his desk; perhaps, too, he should have knocked; so knock he did.

"What d'ye want there, young feller?" shouted a policeman across the street.

"I want to see Mr. Tramlay."

"Guess your watch is slow, ain't it?" growled the officer.

"I don't know: maybe so," Phil replied.

"Don't you know better'n to come huntin' down here for a bizness-man after six o'clock at night?" asked the officer.

Phil admitted to himself that he did not; still, he had come ashore to find Mr. Tramlay, and the idea of giving up the search did not occur to him. He finally asked,—

"Where do you suppose I can find him?"

"At home, I guess, if he's one of the kind that goes straight home from his store."

"I reckon he is," said Phil. "Will you please tell me where he lives?"

"Oh, come off!" muttered the policeman. "D'ye s'pose I ain't got nothin' to do but know where folks live? Where was you brought up?—'way back?"

"I'm sorry I bothered you, sir," said Phil, who now saw the officer's uniform, and recognized it, by memory of pictures he had seen in illustrated newspapers. "Isn't there any way to find out where a man lives in New York?"

"Certainly; look in the Directory. Go up to Broadway,—it's up at the head of this street,—an' go along till you find a drug-store. Like enough you'll find a Directory there."

Phil followed instructions, and learned the street and number of the Tramlay domicile. In front of him street-cars were continually coming and going, and by the conductors of these he was referred from one to another until he found a car which went to the street he wanted to reach. Although Phil knew the city was large, the journey seemed very long; it

c

was made an hour longer than it should have been ; for a fire had broken out somewhere along the route, and engine-hose blockaded the railway-track. When finally the desired street was reached, Phil found himself several hundred numbers away from that he was looking for, and it was then nearly nine o'clock.

"I've half a mind to give it up," said Phil, as he walked rapidly along. "Perhaps they go to bed early : there's no telling. Still, if they're abed I'll know it by the lights being out. I don't seem to walk down these numbers very fast."

He quickened his steps ; he almost ran ; but more than a quarter of an hour passed before he saw on a glass transom the number that indicated his journey was at an end. Phil stopped ; then he crossed the street, and surveyed the house carefully.

"Lights in all the windows," said he. "That looks as if they'd all gone to their own rooms ; looks like bedtime. I was afraid of it. I suppose there's nothing to do but go back to the sloop, or find some place to lodge. Too bad !"

He re-crossed the street, and ascended a step or two : truthful though he was, he would have denied to any one but himself that he did it only because Lucia had tripped up those same steps. Slowly he descended and walked away ; but he had passed but a house or two, and was looking backward, when a man who had passed him ran up the Tramlay steps. Then Phil saw a flash of light and heard a door close.

"That wasn't Mr. Tramlay. There aren't any other men in the family. He must be a visitor.

Well, if other men can call at this time of night, I guess I can visit it too."

Back he went, and, as he was unacquainted with the outer mechanism of door-bells, he rapped sharply upon the door. It opened instantly, and as Phil stepped in he found the hall and stairway, as well as the parlors, quite full of ladies and gentlemen.

"It's a party," he said to himself. Then he informed himself, in great haste, that he would postpone his visit, but as he turned to go he found the door was closed, and a small colored boy who stood by it said, "Gen'lmen fust room back," and pointed up-stairs. Entirely losing his self-possession, and wondering what to do, Phil stood stupidly staring about him, when suddenly he saw Lucia in full evening dress. He hastily dropped his eyes, for he had never before seen a dress of that particular cut.

CHAPTER IV.

"WELL, who hasn't come?" asked Edgar Tramlay, as Lucia hurried toward him with a countenance in which despondency and indignation were striving for mastery. Tramlay knew his daughter's moods, for they were exact duplicates of some he had married a score of years before.

"Oh, if he hadn't come!—if he hadn't come!"

The head of the family looked puzzled; then his expression changed to indignation as he asked,—

"Has any one dared to come to my house after drinking?"

"Worse than that!" wailed Lucia, shuddering, and covering her eyes with her pretty hands. Her father at once strode to the hall-way, looking like an avenging angel; but when he reached the door and took in at a glance the entire cause of his daughter's annoyance he quickly put on a smile, and exclaimed,—

"Why, my dear fellow, how lucky that you happened in town on our reception evening! Come with me; Mrs. Tramlay will be delighted to see you again."

Phil resisted the hand laid upon his arm, and replied,—

36

"I'll call again,—some other time. I didn't know you had company this evening."

"All the better," said the host, leading Phil along; "'twill give you a chance to meet some of our friends. We've met many of yours, you know."

Just then the couple stopped in front of a sofa on which Phil, whose eyes were still cast down, saw the skirts of two or three dresses. Then he heard his escort say,—

"My dear, you remember our old friend Phil Hayn, I'm sure?"

Phil looked up just in time to see Mrs. Tramlay's feeble nervous face twitch into surprise and something like horror. Mr. Tramlay extended his hand, as a hint that his wife should arise,—a hint which could not be ignored after his hand had closed upon hers. Even when upon her feet, however, the lady of the house seemed unable to frame a greeting; had Phil been a city acquaintance, no matter how uninteresting, she would have smiled evasively and told him she was delighted that he had been able to come, but what could a lady, at her own reception, say to a young man in a sack-coat and a hard-rubber watch-guard?

Mrs. Tramlay looked at her husband in weak protest; her husband frowned a little and nodded his head impatiently; this pantomime finally stimulated Mrs. Tramlay to such a degree that she was able to ejaculate,—

"What a delightful surprise!"

"Let me make you acquainted with some of the company," said the host, drawing Phil away. "Don't

4

feel uncomfortable; I'll explain that you just dropped in from out of town, so you couldn't be expected to be in evening dress."

Phil began to recover from his embarrassment, thanks to his host's heartiness, but also to the fact that the strain had been too severe to last long. He slowly raised his eyes and looked about him, assisted somewhat by curiosity as to what "evening dress" meant. He soon saw that all the gentlemen wore black clothes and white ties, and that the skirts of the coats retired rapidly. He had seen such a coat before,—seen it often at Haynton, on Ex-Judge Dickman, who had served two terms in the Legislature and barely escaped going to Congress. The only difference between them was that the judge's swallow-tail coat was blue and had brass buttons,—not a great difference, if one considered the distance of New York and Haynton.

"Upon my word," exclaimed Tramlay, suddenly, "I don't believe you've met Lucia yet. Here she is—daughter?"

Lucia was floating by,—a vision of tulle, ivory, peachblow, and amber; she leaned on the arm of a young man, into whose face she was looking intently, probably as an excuse for not looking at the unwelcome visitor. Her father's voice, however, she had always instinctively obeyed; so she stopped, pouted, and looked defiantly at Phil, who again dropped his eyes, a low bow giving him a pretext.

"Daughter," said Tramlay, "here's our old friend Phil, from Haynton. Now, don't spend the whole evening talking over old times with him, but intro-

duce him to a lot of pretty girls: you know them
better than I. Phil, you can explain to them how
you struck a full-dress reception just after landing
from a cruise; 'twill amuse them more, I'll warrant,
than any story any showy young fellow can tell them
this evening. It isn't every young man who can
have a good thing to tell against himself the first
time he meets a new set."

During the delivery of this long speech Lucia eyed
Phil with boldness and disfavor, but in obedience to
her father she took Phil's arm,—an act that so quickly
improved the young man's opinion of himself that
he instantly felt at ease and got command of such
natural graces as he possessed; he was even enabled
to look down at the golden head by his shoulder and
make some speeches bright enough to cheer Lucia's
face.

"It mayn't be so entirely dreadful, after all,"
thought the girl; "I can introduce him to friends to
whom I could afterward explain,—friends who are
too good-hearted to make spiteful remarks afterward.
Besides, I can blame father for it: all girls have
fathers whose ways are queer in one way or another."

While acting upon this plan, and finding, to her
great relief, that Phil could talk courteous nothings
to new acquaintances, she suddenly found herself
face to face with a man of uncertain age but faultless
dress and manner, who said,—

"Mayn't I be favored with an introduction? Your
friend is being so heartily praised by your father
that I am quite anxious to know him."

"Mr. Marge, Mr. Hayn," said Lucia. Phil's proffered hand was taken by what seemed to be a bit of languid machinery, although encircled at one end by a cuff and coat-sleeve and decorated with a seal-ring. Phil scanned with interest the face before him, for he had often heard Mr. Marge mentioned when the Tramlay family were at Haynton. His look was returned by one that might have been a stare had it possessed a single indication of interest, surprise, or curiosity. Mr. Marge had met young men before; he had been seeing new faces for twenty-five years, and one more or less could not rouse him from the composure which he had been acquiring during all that time.

"Can you spare your friend a few moments?" said Mr. Marge to Lucia. "I would be glad to introduce him to some of the gentlemen."

"You are very kind," murmured Lucia, who was dying—so she informed herself—to rejoin some of her girl friends and explain the awkward nature of the intrusion. Marge offered Phil his arm, a courtesy the young man did not understand, so he took Phil's instead, and presented the youth to several gentlemen as an old friend of the family. Soon, however, Marge led Phil into a tiny room at the rear of the hall,—a room nominally the library, the books consisting of a dictionary and a Bible, the greater part of the shelf-space being occupied by pipes, tobacco-boxes, cigar-cases, ash-receivers, and other appurtenances of the vice and comfort of smoking. Placing Phil in a great easy-chair, the back of which hid him from the company, Marge took a cigarette from his own case, which he afterward passed to Phil.

"No small vices," said he, as Phil declined. "Just as well off, I suppose. As for me,"—here Mr. Marge struck a match,—"I've (puff) been acquainted with the weed so long that (puff) I can't very well snub it when I would."

"I think nicotine is injurious to the brain, the lungs, and finally to the digestion," said Phil. "Have you seen Professor Benchof's analyses? They were printed in the——"

"I may have seen them in print, but I'm sure I passed them," said Marge, exhaling smoke in such a way that it hid his face for an instant. "I can't afford to worry myself with information that I'd rather not use."

"But one's physique——" said Phil.

"One's physique becomes quite obliging when it knows what is expected of it."

Phil mentally sought a way of passing this unexpected obstacle: meanwhile, Marge breathed lazily through his cigarette a moment or two, and then said,—

"Miss Tramlay is a charming girl."

"Indeed she is," Phil replied. "If she only were——"

"Tut, tut, my dear sir," said Marge, "woman is divine, and it isn't good form to criticise divinity. Miss Tramlay is remarkably pretty: I trust we agree at least upon that safe ground?"

"Pretty?" echoed Phil, before Marge had ceased speaking. "She is radiant,—angelic!"

Again Mr. Marge enshrouded his face with smoke, after which he did not continue the conversation,

4*

except to remark, "Yes." Phil studied the color-tone
of the room, and wondered why paper like that on
the wall had not been offered for sale by the store-
keeper at Haynton ; then he resolved he would buy
and take home to his mother a chair just like that in
which he was sitting, for it was so comfortable that
he felt as if he could fall asleep in it. Indeed, he
was already so oblivious to Marge and other human
presence that he was startled when a gentle rustle
ushered in Lucia, who exclaimed,—

"Phil, you must come back to the parlor. Half a
dozen girls are real envious because they haven't seen
you at all, and half a dozen others want to see more
of you. Father has been sounding your praises until
they're sure the Admirable Crichton has come to life
again."

Phil attempted to rise,—an awkward operation to
a man previously unacquainted with Turkish chairs.
Lucia laughed, and offered him assistance : it was
only a little hand, but he took it, and as he looked
his thanks he saw Lucia's face as he had sometimes
known it of old,—entirely alert and merry. At the
same time a load fell from his mind, a load which he
had been vaguely trying to attribute to the lateness
of the hour, the strangeness of his surroundings,—
anything but the manner in which the girl had first
greeted him. As she took his arm and hurried him
out of the library he felt so fully himself that he forgot even that he was not attired like the gentlemen
around him.

Mr. Marge, who had risen when Lucia entered the
library, followed the couple with his eyes ; then, when

alone, he frowned slightly, bit his lip, dropped the end of his cigarette, paced to and fro several times, leaned on the mantel, and muttered,—

"'Phil'!"

Then he lighted another cigarette, and veiled his face in smoke for several minutes.

CHAPTER V.

NOT SO DREADFUL AFTER ALL.

REGULAR hours being among the requirements of the head of the Tramlay household, Lucia appeared at the breakfast-table, the morning after the reception, as the clock struck eight. Her father, dressed for business, and her mother, in *négligée* attire and expression, were discussing the unbidden guest of the evening before.

"But he was so country,—so dreadful common," protested Mrs. Tramlay, with her customary helpless air.

"Nonsense!" said her husband. "There was nothing country or common about his face and manners. There hasn't been so bright-eyed, manly-looking a fellow in our house before since I don't know when. Eh, Lucia?"

"Agnes Dinon said he was real fine-looking," the girl answered.

"Agnes Dinon is thirty-six, if she's a day," said Mrs. Tramlay, in a petulant tone.

"So much the better fitted to pass opinions on young men," said Tramlay. "Shows more sense in one girl of her age than a hundred like—like——"

"Like me, papa," said Lucia. "You may as well say it."

44

"Like you, then. Bless your dear ignorant heart, I'd give my head if you could see as clearly as she without waiting so long to learn."

"You may be very sure, though, that Miss Agnes will never invite him to her own receptions," declared Mrs. Tramlay.

"Wrong again, mamma; she's invited him for next Tuesday night, and I do believe she devised the reception just for the purpose. None of us had heard of it before."

Mrs. Tramlay gathered all her strength, stimulated it with an entire cup of tea, and exclaimed,—

"Well, I should like to know what society is coming to, if a common farmer's boy, of no family, can stumble into town and be invited about to good houses."

"Coming to? Why, my dear wife, it is coming to its senses. I'm glad, in this particular case, the movement began at our house."

"Nobody would have paid any attention to him, if you hadn't talked so much about him," said Mrs. Tramlay. "One would have thought him a dear old friend, to hear you go on about him as you did."

"I said nothing but what was true. I merely said he was one of the finest young men I had ever known,—that he was of the highest character, and very intelligent besides."

"Such qualities don't make a man fit for society," said the lady of the house.

"No, I suppose not; if they did we'd see more of them at our receptions and parties."

"Edgar!"

"Well, well," said Tramlay, leaving the table, kissing his wife, and preparing to hurry to his office, "it isn't your fault; we can't expect what can't be had, I suppose."

"Lucia," said Mrs. Tramlay, after the children had been despatched to school, "I hope your father's peculiar notions won't affect you."

"About Phil? Nonsense, you dear old worry! But, really, mother, he made quite an impression. A lot of the girls admired him ever so much. I began to apologize and explain, as soon as I could get rid of him; but I found it wasn't at all necessary."

"Girls will admire anything that's new,—anything, from a Zulu to a monkey."

"Mamma!"

"Young men like Hayn can't ever marry out of their own circle: you should be able to see that. How can they buy houses for their wives, and furnish them properly, and set up horses and carriages, and keep in society?"

"Mamma, you're too dreadfully funny; indeed you are. Suppose young men aren't rich enough to marry; can't girls like them? Aren't young people good for anything but to get married?"

"I'm very sorry," said the mother, abruptly leaving the room, "that you have such trifling views of life."

When Philip Hayn left the family mansion, a little after midnight, he had but two distinct ideas: one was that he had better find his way back to Sol Mantring's sloop to sleep, and the other was that he didn't believe he could fall asleep again in less than a

week. All that he had seen, the people not excepted,
was utterly unlike Haynton. The conversation, also,
was new, although he could not remember much of it;
and the ladies—well, he always had admired whatever
was admirable in the young women in the village,
but there certainly were no such handsome and brilliant girls at Haynton as some he had met that
night. He could not explain to himself the difference, except that, compared with Lucia's friends,
his old acquaintances appeared—well, rather unfin-
ished and ignorant. And as far as these new acquaintances appeared above his older ones, so far
did Lucia appear above her friends. He had studied
her face scores of times before, and told himself
where it was faulty; now he mentally withdrew
every criticism he had ever made, and declared her
perfection itself. Would he ever forget how she
looked as she offered to help him from that easy-
chair in the library? He wished his mother might
have seen her at that instant; then he was glad she
did not. He remembered that his mother did not
entirely approve of some of Lucia's bathing-dresses;
what would the good woman think of fashionable
evening attire? And yet perhaps it was not as
dreadful as it seemed: evidently Lucia's mother approved of it, and was not she a member of a church,
—not, he regretted, of the faith in which all Haynton worshipped, yet still a church? And did not
many of Lucia's guests dress in similar style?

He mentally laid the subject away for future consideration, and gave his mind to his own attire.
Until that evening his faith in the perfection of his

Sunday suit was as unquestioning as his faith in Haynton's preacher, but now it was hopelessly shattered. He did not admire the attire of the gentlemen he had met, but the evidence was overwhelming that it was the correct thing, and that he must prepare himself to dress in like fashion if he went to Miss Dinon's party. And, by the way, what a queenly woman that Miss Dinon was! He would like to meet her again : he certainly must attend that party. But if he bought evening dress, what should he do with it when he left the city? No young man felt more freedom than he to do as he liked in Haynton, but to appear in a "swallow-tail" at church or anywhere else in the village would be simply impossible : the mere thought of it made him tremble and then laugh. A suit of clothes merely to wear two or three evenings—perhaps only one—would be a shocking extravagance: they probably would cost half as much as a new horse, or two or three dozen of the books he had for years been longing to buy. He would give up Miss Dinon's party: the thought of doing so made him doleful, but do it he must.

Almost immediately after forming this virtuous resolution he boarded a horse-car, on which were several couples, evidently returning from a party somewhere : so again Phil found himself studying attire. Gradually it occurred to him that his own appearance was attracting attention. This was not a new experience: he had encountered it several times at Haynton with calmness ; indeed, although he was not vain, he had never feared comparison, in church, of his appearance with that of any summer boarder from the city; for, as his mother has already intimated in these pages, his Sunday coat had been cut from the same piece of cloth as the minister's. But now he felt ill at ease while being eyed, not at all impertinently, by the young people who sat facing him. First he thought the mildly critical glances were directed to his hard-rubber watch-guard; then he was sure the cut of his vest was not being approved; he detected one very pretty young woman in the act of suppressing a smile as she looked at his shoes. Thirdly, he was obliged to believe that an admirably-dressed fellow opposite entirely disapproved of his Sunday coat,—the coat cut from minister's cloth and made by Sarah Tweege, and with a real silk-velvet collar, too!

Little by little Phil lost his self-possession; he could scarcely look in any direction without encountering the eyes of some one who seemed to regard him as a curiosity. An attempt to ignore the attention by reading the advertising signs above the windows of the car was a dismal failure, for he somehow felt that several pairs of eyes were upon him, and this was rather more annoying than seeing them. The strain became unendurable; so he suddenly looked through a window, as if to see where he was, then hastily went to the rear platform and asked the conductor to let him off. As he stood there he heard a young man whisper,—

"Country!"

Then he heard a young woman softly ejaculate,—

"Te-he!"

The street was as dark as gas-lighted streets usually

c   d   5

are ; it was almost deserted, and the autumn evening
was quite chilly, but Phil felt as if his blazing eyes
were illuminating everything,—as if the walls had
eyes to look disapprovingly at Haynton fashions, or
as if his own blood were hot enough to warm the
entire atmosphere of New York. He knew what he
would do : when he reached Sol Mantring's sloop he
would remain aboard until she sailed ; then he would
go back to Haynton and remain there forever. He
could exist without New York, if New York found
him unsatisfactory. He didn't care ever to see again
anybody in New York, except, perhaps, Lucia. As
for her, hadn't even she——

Before the next car arrived, Phil had entirely
changed his mind. Nevertheless, before continuing
his journey he cautiously peered in to see if any of the
passengers were likely to prove critical. There seemed
to be no one to fear ; at one end of the car was a
shabby-looking peddler with his pack, evidently arrived by a late train from the suburbs ; at the other
an old man seemed inclined to doze, and directly
opposite the newest passenger sat a plain, modest-
looking person, whom a New Yorker would have
rightly identified as a waiter at a restaurant or café.
Apparently three persons less qualified or inclined to
criticise personal appearance could not have been
found by careful search ; yet within five minutes Phil
was sure that all of them had noticed him and studied
him.   As he was disinclined to squander another
car-fare on his feelings, he sought the dusky seclusion
of the rear platform and engaged the conductor in
conversation, which on Phil's part consisted solely

of questions; yet he was astonished, as well as indignant, when the conductor remarked, at a moment
when the talk showed signs of lagging,—

"You're from the rural district, I s'pose?"

"What makes you say that?" asked Phil, indi-
cating a sense of injury.

"Oh, I didn't mean nothin' out of the way," said
the conductor. "I only kinder thought I was sure—
why, I come from the country myself; yes sir, an' I
ain't ashamed of it, neither."

The explanation was not satisfactory; so Phil
completed the trip in gloomy silence, and he felt a
sense of great relief when he reached Sol Mantring's
sloop and made his way into the little cabin, where,
of the three men lying at ease, no one took the pains
to intimate that Phil was anything but city-born and
city-bred.

CHAPTER VI.

RECONSTRUCTION.

PHIL devoted part of the next day to studying well-dressed business-men in the streets. Thanks to well-trained perceptive faculties, and also to some large mirrors which he accidentally encountered, he soon learned why his attire had attracted attention. Then he compared clothing-stores for an hour, finally entered one and asked how long it would take to make a well-fitting every-day suit. The salesman looked him over, and replied,—

"Fit you at once, from our ready-made stock. Never any trouble to fit a good figure."

Phil could have hugged that salesman. Here, at least, was some one who did not intimate that he was from the country; and yet, perhaps, a good figure was a country product. He would think about this, as soon as business was off his mind. The salesman certainly fitted him to perfection. Phil scarcely recognized himself when asked to look in the glass.

"Don't think you could do better," said the veteran salesman, surveying Phil from rapidly-changing points of view, "if you were to have yourself melted and poured into a suit. The tone of that goods is rather cold, but you've plenty of color. I think, though, to set it off to the best advantage you need to

change your black tie for a scarf with a touch of red
or yellow in it: if you don't happen to have one,
you'll find a fine assortment in our gents' furnishing
department. Needs a somewhat different style of
shirt-collar, too: let some furnishing-goods man cast
his eye over your neck. You always wear your hair
pretty long, I suppose?—well, it's a pity it don't set off
a man's clothes as well as it sometimes does his face."

Phil resolved at once to have his hair cut. Under
the guidance of the salesman he had his neck-wear
changed; then the old man said,—

"Those low-crowned straight-brimmed hats used
to look exactly right with the clothes of that season,
but somehow they don't harmonize with the cut of
this year. Hats are cheap, though, and there are two
or three good dealers on the other side of the street,
a little farther down. Keep this suit on, I suppose?
All right, sir: I'll do up the others. H'm!"—here
the old man scrutinized the material of the coat
made by Sarah Tweege,—"that's splendid stuff.
Great shame 'twas cut sack-fashion. There isn't
much stuff as good as that in swallow-tails nowadays."

"Couldn't it—I suppose it couldn't be made over
into a party coat?"

"H'm!—scarcely,—scarcely," said the salesman,
controlling his features as well as if the question
were the most natural in the world. "Not enough
stuff, you see; too short; sleeves not full enough;
button-holes in wrong places; lapels too narrow.
Besides, velvet collars have gone out. Any time you
need a dress-suit, though, we've got a boss artist who

5*

can cut it so as to do you justice. 'Tisn't often he gets a good figure to spread himself on."

Again Phil was profoundly grateful : he wanted to do something for that salesman, and after some thought he astonished the old fellow by thanking him for his attention and promising to send him a barrel of selected Newtown pippins. Then he placed himself in the hands of the boss artist, who studied him as if he were a model, measured him, and asked him if he needed his dress-suit at once.

"Yes ; right away," said Phil. "I can't get it too soon. I want——" He had begun to tell that he meant to dress himself in that suit and practise before a mirror until fully satisfied that he did not look unlike other men. The boss artist told him to return in three days; then the old salesman, who had remained in attendance, remarked,—

" You have a thin fall overcoat, I suppose ?"

"Oh, I won't need an overcoat for a month yet. Why, there hasn't been a bit of frost up our way." Phil was already appalled by the extent of his order.

"True enough," said the salesman, "but it doesn't do to go out in a dress-suit without an overcoat, you know, unless you're merely stepping from your door to a carriage ; and it's hardly the thing even then."

"Why, Judge Dickman——"

"Oh, yes, those old judges, who wear swallow-tails day in and day out, can do it ; nothing wrong about it, of course,—only a matter of taste ; but a young fellow don't like to make himself conspicuous, you know."

Phil meekly purchased an overcoat, and hurried

away with a heavy load on his conscience. More
than three-quarters of the hundred dollars his father
had given him was already gone or mortgaged; he
had meant to spend none of it, except for some things
which he knew his mother craved. Fortunately, he
had brought some savings of his own; and, as he
informed himself, hair-cutting was not an expensive
operation, and the clothing-salesman had told him
that new hats did not cost much. He had nothing
else to spend money for, except a watch-chain; his
father had told him to buy one. Indeed, had not his
father told him to buy clothes?—"lots of them," were
the old gentleman's exact words. But could his father
have known about evening suits and fall overcoats?

Phil continued in this vein of thought after he had
dropped into a barber's chair, but was startled out of
it by finding a lather-brush passing over his face.
He struggled, and exclaimed,—

"I wanted my hair cut."

"Yes, sir, so I heard you say; but when shaving
has to be done too we like to have that out of the way
first. But I beg your pardon, perhaps you were
raising a beard?"

"No," said Phil, settling himself again in the chair.
At Haynton young men shaved only on Saturday
nights; Phil himself had shaved only three days
before, yet here was another unexpected expense
imposed upon him by New York custom. Half an
hour afterward he emerged from that shop with the
not entirely satisfactory assurance that his oldest
friend would not know him at sight: and when he
had bought a new hat and surveyed himself in a

long mirror he was not certain that he would know
himself if he were to encounter another mirror by
accident. The replacement of his hard-rubber watch-
guard by a thin chain plated with gold completed
the metamorphosis, and a bootblack whose services he
declined set his mind at rest by calling him a dude.

What next to do he scarcely knew. An inclination
to go back to the sloop and see how Sol Mantring
was getting along at discharging the cargo was sup-
pressed by the thought of what Sol and the crew
would say if they saw him in his new suit. The
countryman has some grand qualities that denizens
of cities would do well to imitate, but not all his
moral courage can keep him from feeling uncomfortable when first he displays himself in new clothes
to old associates. Country youths have sometimes
run away from home,—gone to sea, the city, the
devil—anywhere—rather than undergo this dreadful
ordeal.

Suddenly it occurred to him that he was not far
from Tramlay's office : he might make a call, if only
to show that he could, with proper facilities, look
unlike a countryman. Besides, he wanted to know
all about the iron business, about which he had seen
so many contradictory assertions in the newspapers.

He entered the store and walked back toward the
railed counting-room in which he saw the head of
Haynton's recent summer boarder. A clerk asked
him his business; he replied that he had merely
dropped in to see Mr. Tramlay. The head of the
establishment looked at Phil without recognition
when this information was imparted, and advanced

with a somewhat impatient air, which suddenly changed to cordiality as he exclaimed,—

"Why, my dear fellow! excuse me. I didn't recognize you at first: we can't all of us have young eyes, you know. Come in; sit down; make yourself at home. I'm glad you dropped in: I'm going out to lunch pretty soon, and I do hate to lunch alone."

Phil soon found himself coaxed and assisted to a high office-stool at a desk by the window, and all the morning papers placed before him, while Tramlay said,—

"Look at the paper two or three minutes while I straighten out a muddle in a customer's letter; then we'll go out."

Phil took up a paper; the advertising page—which happened to be the first—was very interesting, nevertheless Phil's eyes wandered, for his mind was just then curious about the iron trade. He looked around him for indications of the business; but the only bit of iron in sight was a paper-weight on the desk before him. Closer scrutiny was rewarded by the discovery of a bit of angle-iron, a few inches long, lying on a window-sill. In the mean time the proprietor had scribbled a few lines, assorted some papers, and closed his desk by drawing down the top. Then he said,—

"Now let's go in search of peace and comfort."

"I shouldn't think you'd have to leave your office for that," said Phil, who had found the counting-room greatly unlike what he had expected.

"There's no peace where business is going on," Tramlay replied; "although I don't know, after careful thought, of any noisier place than a New York restaurant. Here we are. Come in."

Phil found himself in one of the very large and noisy places where New York business-men herd about noonday. Phil protested, in the usual rural manner, that he was not at all hungry, but Tramlay ordered so skilfully that both were duly occupied for an hour. Phil found his host attentive, yet occasionally absent-minded. He might have spared himself the trouble of making a mental memorandum to study out the why and wherefore of this apparently incongruous pair of qualities had he known that Tramlay was cudgelling his brain to know how to dispose of his rural visitor after dinner, without offending. While they were sipping the coffee,—a beverage which Phil had never before tasted in the middle of the day,—Mr. Marge lounged up to them, looking exactly as intelligent, listless, and unchangeable as the night before.

"How are you, Marge?" said Tramlay. Phil afterward wondered that his host could smile so genially on so cold a person.

"As usual," replied Marge, with a slight inclination of the head. "Good-morning, Mr. Hayn. Don't let me interrupt conversation. I merely meant to say I've nothing to do this afternoon, and would be glad to show Mr. Hayn about town a little, if he likes."

"That's ever so good of you," said Tramlay; "for the truth is, I was wondering how I could find time to do it myself, and fearing I couldn't."

"Entirely at his service," said Marge, as lifelessly as an automaton.

" And both come and dine with me this evening,"
suggested Tramlay : "entirely informal, you know."

" I should be delighted," said Marge, in his un-
varying manner.

Tramlay hurried to his office, after the briefest of
leave-takings, and Marge began to conduct Phil about
New York. Soon, however, there developed a marked
difference of taste between visitor and guide. Marge
wanted to show the young man the Stock Exchange,
which to the many minds composing a very large
class has no rival attraction except the various in-
stitutions on Blackwell's Island ; Phil exhibited ab-
ject ignorance and indifference regarding the Stock
Exchange, but wanted to go through the Sub-Treas-
ury and Assay Office,—two buildings in which
Marge had never been. Marge made a special trip
to show the young man the outside of Jay Gould's
office, but Phil identified Trinity Church from pictures he had seen, and wanted to make a patriotic
tour of the tombs of distinguished men of the Revolutionary period. Marge offered to introduce Phil to
Russell Sage, but was amazed to learn that the young
man had never heard of that distinguished individ-
ual. When, however, General Hancock, passing by,
was casually pointed out by Marge, Phil stopped
short and stared respectfully. Marge showed the
Field Building, but through the trees in front Phil
correctly surmised he saw Castle Garden, and desired
at once to go there and be made acquainted with the
method of receiving and distributing immigrants.
On the Produce Exchange they fairly agreed, Marge
admitting that in importance it ranked next to the

Stock Exchange, while Phil was able to regard it as a great business necessity. Pretending to search, by Phil's request, for the building in which Washington bade farewell to his generals, Marge succeeded in getting back through Broad Street to the vicinity of the Stock Exchange, where he tried to atone for his failure by pointing out through a window the head of Mr. Henry Clews ; but Phil had no eyes except for the statue of Washington, standing, as he knew, on the site of the first President's first inaugural. The two men exhibited equal interest, on half a dozen successive occasions, in " stock-tickers," which Marge seemed to know how to find in all sorts of places; but, while Marge looked over the quotations on the tape, Phil studied the machinery of the indicator itself.

The strain upon Marge became almost too great for his self-control, and he breathed a sigh of relief when Trinity's clock struck three. To have left the vicinity of the Stock Exchange earlier would never have occurred to him, but promptly on the stroke he hurried Phil to an elevated-railway station and up-town to a stable, where he had his horse and wagon brought out and took Phil for a drive in Central Park. Probably there he thought he could be entertained after his own manner, for he had the reins. Driving out Fifth Avenue, the two men really became congenial for a little while, for Phil understood horses, and Marge's horse was a good one, and Phil admired him and knew of a good horse that would match him nicely, and Marge saw a prospect of making a team that he could sell at a large profit,

and Phil promised to arrange that Marge should
come out and see the horse. But even this conversation was broken when Marge pointed out the late
residence of A. T. Stewart, for Phil insisted upon
moralizing on riches. In the Park he asked questions about statues, and about trees and shrubs that
were new to him and equally unknown to Marge, as
well as utterly uninteresting; Phil also wanted a
number of facts and figures about the Reservoir in
the Park, and was with difficulty restrained from
spoiling the drive by visiting the menagerie. Finally,
when he demanded the exact sites of the various engagements on Manhattan Island between the British
and Washington, after the latter had been forced to
evacuate what then was New York, Marge abruptly
turned and drove homeward, confessing without the
faintest show of shame, but rather with defiance,
that he knew absolutely nothing about those times.
And when the drive ended and the couple separated,
the elder man's face broke from its customary calm
as he muttered to himself,—

"What can Tramlay want of that fellow?"

6

CHAPTER VII.

AT HER SIDE.

THE arrangement of the guests at the dinner-table that evening suited all concerned. Phil sat at the right of the host, with Lucia directly opposite, where her face was before him all the while. Marge sat at the right of the hostess, where he could closely observe the young man from the country, and, not less important, Tramlay's manner toward the younger guest. He could also note the effect of the young man and his ways upon Mrs. Tramlay; for did he not know how to translate every expression of her face? It was his own fault if he did not, for he had been one of her suitors nearly a quarter of a century before, and the lady had never ceased to be mildly grateful for this compliment, and to repose as much confidence in him as a loyal wife might without harm grant an acquaintance who never had been offensive.

That Mrs. Tramlay wanted Lucia to become Mrs. Marge was one of these confidences,—not spoken, but none the less distinctly understood,—and it had taken all of Marge's adroitness to maintain his position with the family, since Lucia's "coming out," to avoid being brought to propose. Several years earlier he had fully intended to make

Lucia his own when she should reach marriageable age, and many and acceptable had been the attentions by which he had endeavored to secure the first place in the girl's regard. But somehow as his prospects gradually yet distinctly brightened, the profits of the iron trade as gradually and distinctly waned; Marge was not in the iron trade himself, but Lucia's father was, and bachelors at forty-five generally expect something with a bride besides a father's blessing. What the girl's father thought of him Marge had never taken time to wonder; for if he was satisfactory to his fastidious self, how could he be otherwise to a plodding family man? His social position was good; his name had never been part of a scandal; he had no debts; he never borrowed money; and, although a club man, no one had ever seen him drunk, or heard of his being fond of actresses. If all this did not make a man not merely irreproachable, but highly desirable as a son-in-law, what did parents expect?

The arrangement of seats at the table suited Lucia also. She knew her mother's matrimonial intentions regarding her. She was not in love with Marge, but girls in her set did not think it good form to be very fond of men whom they probably would have to marry. If, however, Marge meant business, she wished he would be more attentive to it. She felt that she was missing a great deal of pleasure for lack of proper escort. Twice in the course of the last season Marge had taken her and her mother to the opera; Lucia adored opera,—that is, she liked to look about the house, and see who was with who, and how the *prima donna* dressed, and to have gentlemen call at her box between acts,—but two operas were merely sips at a cup she longed to drain, and only once had she been able to persuade her father to mitigate the privation. If apparent interest in Phil at table could have any effect upon Marge's languid purpose, the provoking fellow should not lack stimulus. To have to devote herself for a whole hour to one young man, in the long hair and country garb which regained their awkwardness in her mind's eye when her father announced that Phil was coming to dinner, seemed a hard task; but when the young man made his appearance Lucia was so agreeably surprised that what had seemed a task at once became by anticipation a positive pleasure.

The evening soon opened promisingly for Marge, for Phil took soup a second time,—a proceeding which inflicted upon Mrs. Tramlay several moments of uncontrolled annoyance and caused profound silence around the table. But Lucia rapidly recovered; desperate cases required desperate remedies; so she said,—

"Phil, do you remember that dinner you once made us in the grove by the beach?"

"Indeed I do," said Phil. "I never shall forget it." And he told the truth; for Lucia's look of horror when he brought from the fire a piece of board piled high with roasted clams had been one of the few great mental dampers of his life.

"You made us forks from dried twigs," said Lucia. "I kept mine as a memento; it is hanging over my mantel now, with a bow of blue ribbon around it."

Marge frowned perceptibly; Mrs. Tramlay looked horrified; but Phil's face lightened so quickly that Lucia's little heart gave a gay bound.

"Why didn't you ever give a clam-bake on Sunday, —the only day I could be there?" asked Tramlay. "I'd give more for such a meal out of doors than for the best dinner that Delmonico could spread."

"Edgar!" gasped Mrs. Tramlay. It did not reach him, though the look that accompanied it passed in its full force from the foot of the table to the head.

"Why, Sunday," said Phil, with some hesitation, —"Sunday is—Sunday."

"Quite true," said the host. "It is in the country, at least; I wish 'twas so here."

"Edgar," said Mrs. Tramlay, "don't make Mr. Hayn think we are heathens. You know we never fail to go to service on Sunday."

"Yes," said Tramlay; "we're as good Pharisees as any other family in New York."

"And after that dinner in the woods," continued Lucia, "we went for pond-lilies: don't you remember? I do believe I should have been drowned in that awful pond if you hadn't caught me."

Again Marge's brows gathered perceptibly.

"He merely drew her aside from a muddy place," whispered Mrs. Tramlay.

"Well, this is interesting," said Tramlay, at the other end of the table. "Hayn, are there many places out your way where silly girls are likely to be drowned if they are allowed to roam about without a keeper?"

"Quite a number," said Phil, as seriously as if his

6   6*

host expected a list of the Haynton ponds and their relative depths. "For instance, Boddybanks Pond is about——"

"Oh, that was the pond where we went canoeing, —that pond with the funny name! My! I wish I was in that very canoe, on that very pond, this very minute."

"Lucia!" exclaimed Mrs. Tramlay.

"I know 'twas dreadfully impolite to say before company," said Lucia, with a pretty affectation of penitence, "but everybody knows I can't be there, and that 'twould be too cold for comfort; so it doesn't do any harm to wish it. And I *should* like that canoe-trip over again: shouldn't you, Phil?"

"I certainly should," said Phil. "That pond is very pretty in summer, when everything around it is green. There are a great many shades of green there, on account of there being a great variety of trees and bushes. But you wouldn't know the place at this season; and I think it's a great deal prettier. The ground—the water, too—is covered with leaves of bright colors; there are a lot of blazing red swamp maples around it, in spots, and three or four cedar-trees, with poison-ivy vines——"

"Ugh!" ejaculated Mrs. Tramlay.

"Poison-ivy leaves, you know, are the clearest crimson in the fall," Phil continued, "and they're so large and grow so close together that they make a bit of woods look like a splendid sunset."

"Oh, papa!" exclaimed Lucia, clapping her hands, "let's go out to Haynton to-morrow, just for two or three days."

"Lucia," said her mother, severely, "you forget all your engagements for the next few days."

"Her father's own child," said Tramlay. "She forgets everything but the subject before her. She would make a good business-man—if she weren't a girl."

"I saw some couples out canoeing at Mount Desert, last season," drawled Marge. "It seemed to me dreadfully dangerous, as well as very uncomfortable for the lady."

"Oh, our canoe wasn't one of those wretched little things; was it, Phil? 'Twas a great long pond-boat, made of beech bark—"

"Birch," suggested Phil.

"Birch bark, and so heavy that I couldn't upset it, though I tried my hardest."

"Lucia!" The voice was Mrs. Tramlay's, of course.

"Why, mamma, the water wasn't knee-deep; I measured it with the paddle."

Mrs. Tramlay sank back in her chair, and whispered that if the family ever went to the country again she would not dare leave that child out of her sight for a single instant, but she had hoped that a girl twenty years of age would have enough sense not to imperil her own life. As for that farmer fellow, she had supposed he was sensible enough to——

"You wouldn't have tried that trick if I had been in the canoe, Miss Tramlay," said Phil.

"Why not?" asked Lucia: she knew how to look defiant without ceasing to be pretty.

"Well, I would have been responsible for you, you know,—your instructor in navigation, so to speak;

and it's one of the first principles of that art not to take any risk unless something's to be gained by it."

"Good!" exclaimed Tramlay.

"Not bad," assented Marge.

"But I'd have got something if I'd succeeded in upsetting the boat," said Lucia: "I'd have got a ducking."

Then everybody laughed,—everybody but Mrs. Tramlay, who intimated to Marge that Lucia was simply being ruined by her father's indulgence.

The dinner ended, the host and Marge retired to the library to smoke. Phil was invited to accompany them, but Lucia exclaimed,—

"Phil has been too well brought up to have such bad habits. He is going to keep me from feeling stupid, as ladies always do while gentlemen smoke after dinner."

She took Phil's arm and led him to the drawing-room, where the young man soon showed signs of being more interested in the pictures on the wall than in the girl by his side.

"These are very different from the pictures you used to see in our little parlor in Haynton," said Phil. "Different from any in our town, in fact."

"Are they?" said Lucia. "But you might be loyal to home, and insist that yours were unlike any in New York; because they were, you know."

"I didn't suppose they were anything unusual," said Phil, quite innocently.

"Oh, they were, though," insisted Lucia, with much earnestness. "I'm sure you couldn't find one of them in any parlor in New York. Let me see: I

do believe I could name them all, if I were to close
my eyes a moment. There was 'General Taylor at
the Battle of Buena Vista,' 'The Destruction of Je-
rusalem,' the 'Declaration of Independence,' 'Napoleon's Tomb at St. Helena,' 'Rock of Ages,' 'George
Washington,' Peale's 'Court of Death,' 'Abraham
Lincoln and his Family,' and 'Rum's Deadly Upas-
Tree.' There !''

"Your memory is remarkable," said Phil. "I
didn't suppose any one had even noticed our pictures
at all ; for I'm sure they are old-fashioned."

"Old-fashioned things, — why, they're all the
fashion now, don't you know?" said Lucia, with a
pretty laugh.

Phil did not reply, for he was quite overpowered
by what seemed to him the elegance of the Tramlay
pictures. He could easily see that the engravings
were superior in quality to those to which he was accustomed ; he was most profoundly impressed by the
paintings,—real oil paintings, signed by artists some
of whose names he had seen in art-reviews in New
York papers. He studied them closely, one after
another, with the earnestness of the person whose
tastes are in advance of his opportunities : in his
interest he was almost forgetful of Lucia's presence.
But the young woman did not intend to be forgotten,
so she found something to say about each picture
over which Phil lingered.

Among the paintings was one which had been seen,
in the original or replicas, in almost all the picture-
auctions which were frequently held in the New
York business-district for the purpose of fleecing men

who have more money than taste. Sometimes the artist's name is German, oftener French, and occasionally Italian; the figures and background also differ from time to time as to the nationality, and the picture is variably named "The Parting," "Good-By," "Auf Wiedersehen," "Good-Night," or "Adieu," but the canvases all resemble one another in displaying a young man respectfully kissing the hand of a young woman. The Tramlays' copy of this auctioneer's stand-by was called "Adieu," the name being lettered in black on the margin of the frame.

"Why," exclaimed Phil, with the air of a man in the act of making a discovery, "I am sure I have seen a wood engraving of that painting in one of the illustrated papers."

"I don't see why they should do it," said Lucia; "it's dreadfully old-fashioned. People don't say 'adieu' in that way nowadays, except on the stage."

"I thought you said a moment ago that old-fashioned things were all the fashion."

Lucia shrugged her shoulders, and said, "Kissing hands may come in again." Then she raised one of her own little hands slightly and looked at it; Phil's eyes followed hers, and then the young man became conscious of a wish that the old form of salutation might be revived, on special occasions, at least. The thought succeeded that such a wish was not entirely proper, and while he reasoned about it Lucia caught his eye and compelled him to blush,—an act which the young woman perhaps thought pretty, for she immediately imitated it, the imitation being much more graceful and effective than the original. The situation was awkward, and Phil instantly lost his self-possession ; but not so Lucia.

"Here," she said, turning so as to face the wall opposite that on which the mischief-making picture hung, "is papa's favorite picture. He thinks everything of it ; but I say it's simply dreadful."

It certainly was. The centre of the canvas, which was enormous, was filled with several columns and a portion of the entablature of a ruined Greek temple.

"It is as large as all the other pictures combined, you see ; all the lines in it are straight, and there isn't anywhere in it a dress, or a bit of furniture, or even bric-à-brac."

Phil imagined his host must have seen other qualities than those named by Lucia, and he seated himself on a sofa to study the picture in detail. Lucia also sat down, and continued :

"There is color in it, to be sure ; bits of the columns where the light is most subdued are as lovely as—as a real Turkish rug."

Much though Phil had endeavored to keep himself in communication and sympathy with the stronger sentiments of the world outside of Haynton, he had never realized even the outer edge of the mysteries and ecstasies of adoration of old rugs. So Lucia's comparison started him into laughter. The girl seemed surprised and offended, and Phil immediately tumbled into the extreme depths of contrition.

"I beg your pardon," he murmured, quickly. "It was all because of my ignorance. We haven't any Turkish rugs at Haynton, nor any other rugs, except those we lay on floors and use very much as if they were carpets. I ought to have known better, though; for I remember that in Eastern stories, where the rare possessions of Oriental kings and chiefs are spoken of, rugs are always classed with jewels and silks and other beautiful things. Please forgive me."

Half in earnest, half pretending, Lucia continued to appear offended. Phil repeated his confession, and enlarged his explanation. In his earnestness he leaned toward her; Lucia dropped her head a little. Marge, who had finished his cigar, entered the parlor at that instant, and raised his eyebrows,— a motion more significant in a man of his temperament than a tragic start would have been to ordinary flesh and blood. Lucia started and showed signs of embarrassment when she could no longer ignore his presence; Phil merely looked up, without seeming at all discomposed.

"I think, my dear," said Tramlay to his wife, who had been turning the backs of a magazine, "that I'll take our friend around to the club with me for half an hour, just to show him how city men squander their time and keep away from their families. I won't be long gone."

"Oh, papa! right after dinner? We've scarcely seen Phil yet, to ask him any questions."

"Plenty of time for that," the merchant replied. "We'll see him often: eh, Hayn?"

"I shall be delighted," said Phil.

"Suppose you drop him at my club, on your way home?" suggested Marge. "I shall be there."

"Good! thanks: very kind of you. He'll see some

men nearer his own age: all our members are middle-aged and stupid."

"I think it's real mean of you both," said Lucia, with a pretty pout.

Phil looked as if he thought so too. At Haynton it was the custom, when one went out to dinner,—or supper, which was the evening meal,—to spend the evening with the entertainer. But objection seemed out of place: the merchant had gone for his hat and coat, and Marge made his adieus and was donning his overcoat at the mirror in the hall.

"I'm very sorry to go," said Phil to Lucia. His eyes wandered about the room, as if to take a distinct picture of it with him: they finally rested on the picture of "The Adieu."

"You shall take my forgiveness with you," said the girl, "if you will solemnly promise never, never to laugh at me again."

"I never will," said Phil, solemnly; then Lucia laughed and offered him her hand. Perhaps it was because Phil had just removed his eyes from "The Adieu" and was himself about to say good-by, that he raised the little hand to his lip. Fortunately for her own peace of mind, Mrs. Tramlay did not see the act, for she had stepped into the library to speak to her husband; Marge, however, was amazed at what he saw in the mirror, and, a second or two later, at Phil's entire composure. Lucia's manner, however, puzzled him; for she seemed somewhat disconcerted, and her complexion had suddenly become more brilliant than usual.

CHAPTER VIII.

HIMSELF FOR COMPANY.

FOR years Philip Hayn had been wondering about the great city only a hundred or two miles distant from his home,—wondering, reading, and questioning,—until he knew far more about it than thousands of men born and reared on Manhattan Island. He had dreamed of the day when he would visit the city, and had formed plans and itineraries for consuming such time as he hoped to have, changing them again and again to conform to longer or shorter periods. He was prepared to be an intelligent tourist, to see only what was well worth being looked at, and to study much that could not be seen in any other place which he was ever likely to visit.

At last he was in New York: his time would be limited only by the expense of remaining at hotel or boarding-house. Yet he found himself utterly without impulse to follow any of his carefully-perfected plans. He strolled about a great deal, but in an utterly aimless way. He passed public buildings which he knew by sight as among those he had intended to inspect, but he did not even enter their doors; the great libraries in which for years he had hoped to quench the literary thirst that had been little more than tantalized by the collective books in

74

Haynton were regarded with impatience. Of all he saw while rambling about alone, nothing really fixed his attention but the contents of shop-windows. He could not pass a clothing-store without wondering if some of the goods he saw within would not become him better than what he was wearing; he spent hours in looking at displays of dress-goods and imagining how one or other pattern or fabric would look on Lucia; and he wasted many hours more in day-dreams of purchasing—only for her—the bits of jewelry and other ornaments with which some windows were filled.

Loneliness increased the weakening effect of his imaginings. He knew absolutely no one in the city but the Tramlays and Marge, and he had too much sense to impose himself upon them; besides, Marge was terribly uninteresting to him, except as material for a study of human nature,—material that was peculiarly unattractive when such a specimen as Lucia was always in his mind's eye and insisting upon occupying his whole attention.

His loneliness soon became intolerable; after a single day of it he hurried to the river, regardless of probable criticism and teasing based on his new clothes, to chat with Sol Mantring and the crew of the sloop. The interview was not entirely satisfactory, and Phil cut his visit short, departing with a brow full of wrinkles and a heart full of wonder and indignation at the persistency with which Sol and both his men talked of Lucia Tramlay and the regard in which they assumed Phil held her. How should they imagine such a thing? He well knew—and

detested—the rural rage for prying into the affairs
of people, particularly young men and women who
seemed at all fond of one another; but what had he
ever done or said to make these rough fellows think
Lucia was to him anything but a boarder in his
father's house? As he wondered, there came to his
mind a line which he had often painfully followed in
his copy-book at school: "The face of youth is an
open book." It did not tend at all to restore composure to his own face.

Hour by hour he found himself worse company.
He had never before made such a discovery. There
had been hundreds and thousands of days in his life
when from dawn to dark he had been alone on the
farm, in the woods, or in his fishing-boat, several
miles off shore on the ocean; yet the companionship
of his thoughts had been satisfactory. He had sung
and whistled by the hour, recited to himself favorite
bits of poetry and prose, rehearsed old stories and
jokes, and enjoyed himself so well that sometimes he
was annoyed rather than pleased when an acquaintance would appear and insist on diverting his attention to some trivial personal or business affair. Why
could he not cheer himself now?—he who always
had been the life and cheer of whatever society he
found himself in?

He tried to change the current of his thoughts by
looking at other people; but the result was dismal in
the extreme. He lounged about Broadway, strolled
in Central Park, walked down Fifth Avenue, and
from most that he saw he assumed that everybody
who was having a pleasant time, driving fine horses,

or living in a handsome house, was rich. He had been carefully trained in the belief that "a man's life consisteth not in the abundance of the things which he possesseth," but his observations of New York were severely straining his faith. He was entirely orthodox in his belief as to the prime source of riches, but he suddenly became conscious of an unhappy, persistent questioning as to why he also had not been born rich, or had riches thrust upon him. He understood now the mad strife for wealth which he had often heard alluded to as the prevailing sin of large cities; he wished he knew how to strive for it himself,—anywhere, in any way, if only he might always be one of the thousands of people who seemed to wear new clothes all the time, and spend their evenings in elegant society, or in the gorgeous seclusion of palaces like that occupied by Marge's club.

For instance, there was Marge. Phil had asked Tramlay what business Marge was in, and the reply was, "None in particular: lives on his income." What, asked Phil of himself, was the reason that such a man, who did not seem much interested in anything, should have plenty of money and nothing to do, when a certain other person, who could keenly enjoy, and, he believed, honestly improve, all of Marge's privileges, should have been doomed to spend his life in hard endeavor to wrest the plainest food from the jealous earth and threatening sea, and have but a chance glimpse of the Paradise that the rich were enjoying,—a glimpse which probably would make his entire after-life wretched. Could he ever again be what he had so long been?—a cheerful, contented young farmer and fisherman? He actually shivered as he called up the picture of the long road, alternately dusty and muddy, that passed his father's house, its sides of brown fence and straggling bushes and weeds converging in the distance, an uncouth human figure or a crawling horse and wagon its only sign of animation, and contrasted it with Fifth Avenue, its boundaries handsome houses and its roadway thronged with costly equipages bearing well-dressed men and beautiful women. Passing the house of a merchant prince, he saw in the window a fine bronze group on a stand; how different from the little plaster vase of wax flowers and fruits which had been visible through his mother's "best room" window as long as he could remember!

Yes, money was the sole cause of the difference: money, or the lack of it, had cursed his father, as it now was cursing him. None of the elderly men he saw had faces more intelligent than his father, yet at that very moment the fine old man was probably clad in oft-patched trousers and cotton shirt, digging muck from a black slimy pit to enrich the thin soil of the wheat-lot. And his mother: it made his blood boil to think of her in faded calico preparing supper in the plain old kitchen at home, while scores of richly-clad women of her age, but without her alert, smiling face, were leaning back in carriages and seemingly unconscious of the blessing of being exempt from homely toil.

And, coming back to himself, money, or lack of it, would soon banish him from all that now his eye was feasting upon. It would also banish him from Lucia. He had read stories of poor young men whom wondrous chances of fortune had helped to the hands and hearts of beautiful maidens clad in fine raiment and wearing rare gems, but he never had failed to remind himself that such tales were only romances; now the memory of them seemed only to emphasize the sarcasm of destiny. Money had made between him and Lucia a gulf as wide as the ocean,—as the distance between the poles,— as——

He might have compared it with eternity, had not his eye been arrested by somebody in a carriage in the long line that was passing up the avenue. It was Lucia herself, riding with her mother. Perhaps heaven had pity on the unhappy boy, for some obstruction brought the line to a halt, and Phil, stepping from the sidewalk, found that the gulf was not too wide to be spanned, for an instant at least, by two hands.

CHAPTER IX.

NEWS, YET NO NEWS.

"Any letters?"

"Not a letter."

"Sho!"

Farmer Hayn and his wife would have made good actors, if tested by their ability to clothe a few words with pantomime of much variety and duration. From almost the time that her husband started to the post-office, Mrs. Hayn had been going out on the veranda to look for him returning. She had readjusted her afternoon cap several times, as she would have done had she expected a visitor; she had picked faded buds from some late roses, had examined the base of one of the piazza posts to be sure that the old wistaria vine was not dragging it from its place, and had picked some bits of paper from the little grass-plot in front of the house; but each time she went from one duty to another she shaded her eyes and looked down the road over which her husband would return. She had eyes for everything outside the house,—an indication of rot at an end of one of the window-sills, a daring cocoon between two slats of a window-blind, a missing screw of the door-knob,—all trifles that had been as they were for weeks, but had failed to attract her attention until expectation had sharpened her eyesight. As time wore on, she went into the house for her spectacles; generally she preferred to have letters read to her by her husband, but her absent son's writing she must see with her own eyes. Then she polished the glasses again and again, trying them each time by gazing down the road for the bearer of the expected letter. Calmness, in its outward manifestation, was noticeable only after her hope had again been deferred.

As for the old man, who was quite as disappointed as his wife, he studied a partly-loosened vest-button as if it had been an object of extreme value; then he sat down on the steps of the veranda, studied all visible sections of the sky for a minute or two, and finally ventured the opinion that a middling lively shower might come due about midnight. Then he told his wife of having met the minister, who had not said anything in particular, and of a coming auction-sale of which he had heard, and how eggs for shipment to the city had "looked up" three cents per dozen. Then he sharpened his pocket-knife on his boot-leg, handling it as delicately and trying its edge as cautiously as if it were an instrument of which great things were expected. Then both joined in estimating the probable cost of raising the youngest calf on the farm to its full bovine estate.

Finally, both having thoroughly repressed and denied and repulsed themselves, merely because they had been taught in youth that uncomfortable restraint was a precious privilege and a sacred duty, Mrs. Hayn broke the silence by exclaiming,—

"It does beat all."

f

"What does?" asked her husband, as solicitously as if he had not the slightest idea of what was absorbing his wife's thoughts.

"Why, that Phil don't write. Here's everybody in town tormentin' me to know when he's comin' back, an' if he's got the things they asked him to buy for 'em, an' not a solitary word can I say ; we don't even know how to send a letter to him to stir him up an' remind him that he's got parents."

"Well, ther's sure to be a letter somewheres on the way, I don't doubt, tellin' us all we want to know," said the old man, going through the motions of budding an althea-bush, in the angle of the step, from a scion of its own stock. "'Watched pots never bile,' you know, an' 'tain't often one gets a letter till he stops lookin' for it."

"But 'tain't a bit like Phil," said the old lady. "Why, he's been away more'n a week. I thought he'd at least let us know which of the big preachers he heerd on Sunday, an' what he thought of 'em. Hearin' them big guns of the pulpit was always one of the things he wanted to go to the city for. Then there's the bread-pan I've been wantin' for ten years,—one that's got tin enough to it not to rust through every time there comes a spell of damp weather : he might at least rest my mind for me by lettin' me know he'd got it."

"All in good time, old lady ; let's be patient, an' we'll hear all we're waitin' for. Worry's more wearyin' than work. Rome wasn't built in a day, you know."

"For mercy's sake, Reuben, what's Rome got to do

with our Phil? I don't see that Rome's got anythin'
to do with the case, onless it's somethin' like New
York, where our boy is."

"Well, Rome was built an' rebuilt a good many
times, you see, 'fore it got to be all that was 'xpected
of it: an' our Phil's goin' through the same operation,
mebbe. A man's got to be either a stupid savage or
a finished-off saint to be suddenly pitched from fields
and woods into a great big town without bein'
dazed. When *I* first went down to York, my eyes
was kept so wide open that I couldn't scarcely open
my mouth for a few days, much less take my pen in
hand, as folks say in letters. I hardly knowed which
foot I was standin' on, an' sometimes I felt as if the
ground was gone from under me. Yet New York
ground is harder than an onbeliever's heart."

Mrs. Hayn seemed to accept the simile of Rome's
building as applied to her son, for she made no further objection to it ; she continued, however, to polish
her glasses, in anticipation of what she still longed to
do with them. Her husband continued to make tiny
slits and cross-cuts in the althea's bark, and to in-
sert buds carefully cut from the boughs. Finally
he remarked, as carelessly as if talking about the
weather,—

"Sol Mantring's sloop's got back."

"Gracious!" exclaimed Mrs. Hayn ; "why ain't
you told me so before? Sol's seen Phil, ain't he?
What does he say? Of course you didn't come home
without seein' him ?"

"Of course I didn't. Yes, Sol's seen Phil,—seen
him the day before he caught the tide an' came out.

An' Sol says he's a stunner, too,—don't look no more like his old self than if he'd been born an' raised in York. I tell you, Lou Ann, it don't take that boy much time to catch on to whatever's got go to it. Why, Sol says he's got store-clothes on, from head to foot. That ain't all, either; he——" Here the old man burst into laughter, which he had great difficulty in suppressing; after long effort, however, he continued: "Sol says he carries a cane,—a cane not much thicker than a ramrod. Just imagine our Phil swingin' a cane if you can!" And the old man resumed his laughter, and gave it free course.

"Mercy sakes!" said the old lady; "I hope he didn't take it to church with him. An' I hope he won't bring it back here. What'll the other members of the Young People's Bible-Class say to see such goin's-on by one that's always been so proper?"

"Why, let him bring it: what's a cane got to do with Bible-classes? I don't doubt some of the 'postles carried canes; I think I've seed 'em in pictures in the Illustrated Family Bible. I s'pose down in Judee ther' was snakes an' dogs that a man had to take a clip at with a stick, once in a while, same as in other countries."

"What else did Sol say?" asked the mother.

"Well, he didn't bring no special news. He said Phil didn't know he was leavin' so soon, else like enough he'd have sent some word. He said Phil was lookin' well, an' had a walk on him like a sojer in a picture. I'm glad the boy's got a chance to get the plough-handle stoop out of his shoulders for a few days. Sez you wouldn't know his face, though, 'cause his hair's cut so short; got a new watch-chain, too; I'm glad to hear that, 'cause I was particular to tell him to do it."

"Well, I half wish Sol Mantring's sloop had stayed down to York, if that's all the news it could bring," said Mrs. Hayn, replacing her spectacles in their tin case, which she closed with a decided snap. "Such a little speck of news is only aggravatin': that's what 'tis."

"Small favors thankfully received, old lady, as the advertisements sometimes say. Oh, there was one thing more Sol said: 'twas that he reckoned Phil was dead gone on that Tramlay gal."

Mrs. Hayn received this information in silence; her husband began to throw his open knife at a leaf on one of the veranda steps.

"I don't see how Sol Mantring was to know anything like that," said Mrs. Hayn, after a short silence. "He isn't the kind that our Phil would go an' unbosom to, if he had any such thing to tell, which it ain't certain he had."

"Young men don't always have to tell such things, to make 'em known," suggested the farmer. "Pooty much everybody knowed when *I* was fust gone on you, though I didn't say nothin' to nobody, not even to the gal herself."

"If it's so," said Mrs. Hayn, after another short pause, "mebbe it explains why he hain't writ. He'd want to tell us 'fore anybody else, an' he feels kind o' bashful like."

"You've got a good mem'ry, Lou Ann," said the old farmer, rising, and pinching his wife's ear.

" What do you mean, Reuben?"

"Oh, nothin', 'xcept that you hain't forgot the symptoms,—that's all."

"Sho!" exclaimed the old lady, giving her husband a push, though not so far but that she was leaning on his shoulder a moment later. "'Twould be kind o' funny if that thing was to work, though, wouldn't it?" she continued; "that is, if Sol's right."

"Well," replied her husband, with a sudden accession of earnestness in his voice, "if Sol's right, 'twon't be a bit funny if it *don't* work. I hope the blessed boy's got as much good stuff in him as I've always counted on. The bigger the heart, the wuss it hurts when it gets hit; an' there's a mighty big heart in any child of you an' me, though I say it as mebbe I shouldn't."

" *That* boy ain't never goin' to have no heart-aches, —not on account o' gals," said the mother, whose voice also showed a sudden increase of earnestness. "I don't b'lieve the gal was ever made that could say no to a splendid young feller like that,—a young feller that's han'some an' good an' bright an' full o' fun, an' that can tell more with his eyes in a minute than a hull sittin'-room-full of ord'nary young men can say with their tongues in a week."

"No," said the old man, soberly, "not if the gal stayed true to the pattern she was made on,—like you did, for instance. But gals is only human,— ther' wouldn't be no way of keepin' 'em on earth if they wasn't, you know,—an' sometimes they don't do 'xactly what might be expected of 'em."

"That Tramlay gal won't give *him* the mitten, anyhow," persisted Mrs. Hayn. "Mebbe she ain't as smart as some, but that family, through an' through, has got sense enough to know what's worth havin' when they see it. She needn't ever expect to come back here to board for the summer, if she cuts up any such foolish dido as that."

"Lou Ann," said the farmer, solemnly, "do you reely think it over an' above likely that she'd *want* to come back, in such case made an' pervided?"

Then both old people laughed, and went into the house, and talked of all sorts of things that bore no relation whatever to youth or love or New York. They retired early, after the manner of farm-people in general, after a prayer containing a formal and somewhat indefinite petition for the absent one. The old lady lay awake for hours, it seemed to her, her head as full of rosy dreams as if it were not covered with snow ; yet when at last she was dropping asleep she was startled by hearing her husband whisper,—

"Father in heaven, have pity on my poor boy."

CHAPTER X.

AGNES DINON'S PARTY.

THROUGH several days spent listlessly except when
dolefully, and through several restless nights, Philip
Hayn was assisted by one hope that changed only to
brighten: it was that nearer and nearer came the
night of the party to which Miss Agnes Dinon had
invited him,—the party at which he was sure he
would again meet Lucia. Except for the blissful incident of the arrested drive on the Avenue, he had
not seen her since the evening when he had raised
her hand to his lips. How the thought of that
moment sent the blood leaping to his own finger-tips!
He had haunted the Avenue every afternoon, not
daring to hope that the carriage would again be
stopped in its course, but that at least he might see
her passing face. As quick as a flash that day his
eye, trained in country fashion to first identify approaching riders by their horses, had scanned the
animals that drew the carriage, so that he might
know them when next he saw them. But again and
again was he disappointed, for spans on which he
would have staked his reputation as being the same
were drawing carriages that did not contain the face
he sought. He might have been spared many heart-
sinkings, as well as doubts of his horse-lore, had he

known that the Tramlays did not keep a turn-out,
but had recourse to a livery-stable when they wanted
to drive.

He had even sought Lucia at church. He had
known, since the family's summer at Haynton, the
name of the church which they attended, and thither
he wended his way Sunday morning; but their pew
was apparently farther back than the seat to which
he was shown, for not one member of the Tramlay
family could he see in front or to either side of him,
and when the service ended and he reached the sidewalk as rapidly as possible he soon learned that the
custom of rural young men to stand in front of
churches to see the worshippers emerge was not
followed at fashionable temples in the city.

Another comforting hope, which was sooner lost
in full fruition, was in the early arrival of his dress-
suit. Fully-arrayed, he spent many hours before
the mirror in his room at the hotel, endeavoring to
look like some of the gentlemen whom he had seen
at the Tramlay reception. Little though he admired
Marge on general principles, he did not hesitate to
conform himself as nearly as possible to that gentleman's splendid composure. Strolling into a theatre
one evening on a "general admission" ticket, which
entitled him to the privilege of leaning against a
wall, he saw quite a number of men in evening dress,
and he improved the opportunity to study the com-
parative effects of different styles of collars and shirt-
fronts. Finally he ventured to appear at the theatre
in evening dress himself, and from the lack of special
attention he justly flattered himself that he did not

carry himself unlike other men. He also made the important discovery that Judge Dickman's custom of buttoning his swallow-tailed coat at the waist, and displaying a yellow silk handkerchief in the fulness thereof, had been abandoned in the metropolis.

At last the long-hoped-for evening arrived, and Phil was fully dressed and uncomfortable before sunset. He had already learned, by observation, that well-dressed men kept their faces closely shaved, and he had experimented, not without an inward groan at his extravagance, in what to him were the mysteries of hair-dressing. He ventured into the streets as soon as darkness had fairly fallen, made his way to the vicinity of the Dinon residence, and from a safe distance reconnoitred the house with the purpose, quite as common in the country as in town, of not being among the earliest arrivals. So long did he watch without seeing even a single person or carriage approach the door that there came to him the horrible fear that perhaps for some reason the affair had been postponed. About nine o'clock, however, his gaze was rewarded by a single carriage ; another followed shortly, and several others came in rapid succession : so a quarter of an hour later he made his own entry. On this occasion he was not unable to translate the instructions, as to the locality of the gentlemen's dressing-room, imparted by the servant at the door ; but, having reached the general receptacle of coats, hats, and sticks, he was greatly puzzled to know why a number of gentlemen were standing about doing nothing. By the time he learned that most of them were merely waiting for their respective feminine charges to descend with them, a clock in the room struck ten, and as Phil counted the strokes and remembered how often he had been half roused from his first doze beneath his bedclothes at home by just that number, he yawned by force of habit and half wished he never had left Haynton.

But suddenly drowsiness, melancholy, and everything else uncomfortable disappeared in an instant, and heaven—Phil's own, newest heaven—enveloped the earth, for as he followed two or three bachelors who were going down-stairs he heard a well-known voice exclaiming,—

"Oh, Phil! Isn't this nice? Just as if you'd been waiting for me! I haven't any escort to-night, so you'll have to take me down. Papa will drop in later, after he's tired of the club."

Oh, the music in the rustle of her dress as it trailed down the stair! Oh, the gold of her hair, the flush of her cheek, the expectancy in her eyes and her parted lips! And only twenty steps in which to have it all to himself! Would they had been twenty thousand!

At the foot of the stair Lucia took Phil's arm, and together they saluted their hostess. Phil felt that he was being looked at by some one besides Miss Dinon, as indeed he was, for handsome young strangers are quite as rare in New York as anywhere else in the world. Nevertheless his consciousness was not allowed to make him uncomfortable, for between long-trained courtesy and intelligent admiration Miss Dinon was enabled to greet him so cordially that he

was made to feel entirely at ease. Other guests came
down in a moment, and Lucia led Phil away, pre-
senting him to some of her acquaintances and keenly
enjoying the surprise of those who recognized in him
the awkward country-boy of a week before. Then
one gentleman after another engaged Lucia in conversation, and begged dances; other ladies with
whom he was chatting were similarly taken from
him; and Phil finally found himself alone on a sofa,
in a position from which he could closely observe the
hostess.

Miss Agnes Dinon was very well worth looking at.
Mrs. Tramlay may not have been far from right in
fixing her years at thirty-six, but there were scores
of girls who would gladly have accepted some of
her years if they might have taken with them her
superb physique and some of the tact and wit that
her years had brought her. Gladly, too, would they
have shared Miss Dinon's superfluous age could they
have divided with her the fortune she had in her
own right. Nobody knew exactly how much it was,
and fancies on the subject differed widely; but what
did that matter? The leading and interesting fact
was that it was large enough to have attracted a
pleasing variety of suitors, so that there had not
been a time since she "came out" when Miss Dinon
might not have set her wedding-day had she liked.
What detriment is there in age to a girl who can
afford to choose instead of be chosen? Is not the full-
blown rose more satisfactory, to many eyes, than the
bud? And how much more charming the rose whose
blushing petals lack not the glint of gold!

Phil had about reached the conclusion that Miss Dinon was a woman whom he believed it would do his mother good to look at, when his deliberations were brought to an end by the lady herself, who approached him and said,—

"At last I can take time to present you to some of my friends, Mr. Hayn. May I have your arm?"

Phil at once felt entirely at ease. It was merely a return of an old and familiar sensation, for he had always been highly esteemed by the more mature maidens of Haynton, and generally found them far more inspiring company than their younger sisters. Phil informed himself, in the intervals of introductions, that Miss Dinon was not like Lucia in a single particular, but she certainly was a magnificent creature. Her features, though rather large, were perfect, her eye was full of soul, especially when he looked down into it, as from his height he was obliged to, and the pose of her head, upon shoulders displayed according to the prevailing custom of evening dress, was simply superb. She found opportunities to chat a great deal, too, as they made the tour of the parlors, and all she said implied that her hearer was a man of sense, who did not require to be fed alternately upon the husks and froth of polite conversation. Phil's wit was quite equal to that of his fair entertainer, and as her face reflected her feelings the guests began to be conscious that their hostess and the stranger made a remarkably fine-looking couple.

Impossible though he would have imagined it half an hour before, Phil's thoughts had been entirely destitute of Lucia for a few moments; suddenly, however, they recovered her, for looking across the head of a little rosebud to whom he had just been introduced, Phil beheld Lucia looking at him with an expression that startled him. He never before had seen her look that way,—very sober, half blank, half angry. What could it mean? Could she be offended? But why? Was he not for the moment in charge of his hostess, who, according to Haynton custom, and probably custom everywhere else, had supreme right when she chose to exercise it?

Could it be—the thought came to him as suddenly as an unexpected blow—could it be that she was jealous of his attention to Miss Dinon, and of his probably apparent enjoyment of that lady's society? Oh, horrible, delicious thought! Jealousy was not an unknown quality at Haynton: he had observed its development often and often. But to be jealous a girl must be very fond of a man, or at least desirous of his regard. Could it be that Lucia regarded him as he did her? Did she really esteem him as more than a mere acquaintance? If not, why that strange look?

If really jealous, Lucia soon had ample revenge, for music began, and Miss Dinon said,—

"Have you a partner for the quadrille, Mr. Hayn? If not, you must let me find you one."

"I—no, I don't dance," he stammered.

"How unfortunate—for a dozen or more girls this evening!" murmured Miss Dinon. "You will kindly excuse me, that I may see if the sets are full?"

Phil bowed, and edged his way to a corner, where in solitude and wretchedness he beheld Lucia go through a quadrille, bestowing smiles in rapid succession upon her partner, who was to Phil's eyes too utterly insignificant to deserve a single glance from those fairest eyes in the world. His lips hardened as ·he saw Lucia occasionally whirled to her place by the arm of her partner boldly encircling her waist. He had always thought dancing was wrong; now he knew it. At Haynton the young people occasionally went through a dance called "Sir Roger de Coverley," but there was no hugging in that. And Lucia did not seem at all displeased by her partner's familiarity,—confound it!

He had to unbend and forget his anger when the quadrille ended, for a pretty maiden to whom he had been introduced accosted him and said some cheerful nothings, fluttering suggestively a miniature fan on which were pencilled some engagements to dance. But soon the music of a waltz arose, and Phil's eye flashed, to a degree that frightened the maiden before him, for directly in front of him, with a man's arm permanently about her slender waist and her head almost pillowed on her partner's shoulder, was Lucia. More dreadful still, she seemed not only to accept the situation, but to enjoy it; there was on her face a look of dreamy content that Phil remembered having seen when she swung in a hammock at Haynton. He remembered that then he had thought it angelic, but—then there was no arm about her waist.

The pretty maiden with the fan had looked to see what had affected the handsome young man so unpleasantly. "Oh," she whispered, "he *is* dreadfully awkward. I positively shiver whenever he asks me for a dance."

"Awkward, indeed!" exclaimed Phil. A very young man with a solemn countenance came over just then to remind the maiden with the fan that the next quadrille would be his: so she floated away, bestowing upon Phil a parting smile far too sweet to be utterly wasted, as it was.

"You seem unhappy, Mr. Hayn," said Miss Dinon, rejoining Phil. "I really believe it's because you don't dance. Confess, now."

"You ought to be a soothsayer, Miss Dinon, you are so shrewd at guessing," said Phil, forcing a smile and then mentally rebuking himself for lying.

"Won't you attempt at least a quadrille? The next one will be very easy."

"Phil!" exclaimed Lucia, coming up to him with an odd, defiant look, part of which was given to Miss Dinon, "you're too mean for anything. You haven't asked me for a single dance."

Phil's smile was of the sweetest and cheeriest as he replied,—

"Wouldn't it be meaner to ask for what I wouldn't know how to accept? We country-people don't know how to dance."

"But any one can go through a quadrille: it's as easy as walking."

"You couldn't have a better opportunity than the next dance, Mr. Hayn," said Miss Dinon, "nor a more graceful partner and instructor than Miss Tramlay."

Lucia looked grateful and penitent; then she took

Phil's arm, and whispered rapidly, "We'll take a side: all you need do will be to watch the head couples carefully, and do exactly as they do, when our turn comes."

"But if I blunder——"

"Then I'll forgive you. What more can you ask?"

"Nothing," said Phil, his heart warming, and his face reflecting the smile that accompanied Lucia's promise. The quadrille was really as easy as had been promised: indeed, Phil found it almost identical, except in lack of grace, with an alleged calisthenic exercise which a pious teacher had once introduced in Haynton's school. The motion of swinging a partner back to position by an encircling arm puzzled him somewhat, as he contemplated it, but Lucia kindly came to his assistance, and 'twas done almost before he knew it,—done altogether too quickly, in fact. And although he honestly endeavored to analyze the wickedness of it, and to feel horrified and remorseful, his mind utterly refused to obey him.

"There!" exclaimed Lucia, as the quadrille ended, and, leaning on Phil's arm, she moved toward a seat. "You didn't seem to find that difficult."

"Anything would be easy, with you for a teacher," Phil replied.

"Thanks," said Lucia, with a pretty nod of her head.

"And I'm ever so much obliged to Miss Dinon for urging me to try," continued Phil.

"Agnes Dinon is a dear old thing," said Lucia, fanning herself vigorously.

"Old?" echoed Phil. "A woman like Miss Dinon can never be old."

r   *g*   9

Lucia's fan stopped suddenly; again the strange jealous look came into her face, and she said,—

"I should imagine you had been smitten by Miss Dinon."

"Nonsense!" Phil exclaimed, with a laugh. "Can't a man state a simple fact in natural history without being misunderstood?"

"Forgive me," said Lucia, prettily. "I forgot that you were always interested in the deepest and most far-away side of everything. Here comes that stupid little Laybrough, who has my next waltz. I'm going to depend upon you to take me down to supper. By-by."

A minute later, and Phil sobered again, for again Lucia was floating about the room with a man's arm around her waist. Phil took refuge in philosophy, and wondered whether force of habit was sufficient to explain why a lot of modest girls, as all in Miss Dinon's parlors undoubtedly were, could appear entirely at ease during so immodest a diversion. During the waltz he leaned against a door-casing : evidently some one was occupying a similar position on the other side, in the hall, for Phil distinctly heard a low voice saying,—

"Wouldn't it be great if our charming hostess were to set her cap for that young fellow from the country?"

"Nonsense!" was the reply : "she's too much the older to think of such a thing."

"Not a bit of it. She'll outlive any young girl in the room. Besides, where money calls, youth is never slow in responding."

"They say he's as good as engaged to Miss Tramlay," said the first speaker.

"Indeed? Umph! Not a bad match. Has he got
any money? I don't believe Tramlay is more than
holding his own."

Phil felt his face flush as he moved away. He
wanted to resent the remarks about his hostess, an
implication that his friend Tramlay was other than
rich, and, still more, that any young man could be
led to the marriage-altar merely by money. If people
were talking about him in such fashion he wished he
might be out of sight. He would return at once to
his hotel, had he not promised to take Lucia down
to supper. He could at least hide himself, for a little
while, in the gentlemen's room up-stairs. Thither
he went, hoping to be alone, but he found Marge,
who had just come in, and who lost his self-possession for an instant when he recognized the well-
dressed young man before him.

"Anybody here?" drawled Marge.

"Lucia is,—I mean Miss Tramlay," said Phil, in
absent-minded fashion,—"and lots of other people,
of course."

Marge looked curiously at Phil's averted face, and
went down-stairs. Phil remained long enough to
find that his mind was in an utter muddle, and that
apparently nothing would compose it but another
glimpse of Lucia. As supper was served soon after
he went down, his wish was speedily gratified.
From that time forward his eye sought her continually, although he tried to speak again to every one
to whom he had been introduced. How he envied

Lucia's father, who was to escort the little witch home! How he wished that in the city, as at Haynton, people walked home from parties, and stood a long time at the gate, when maid and man were pleasantly acquainted!

He saw Lucia go up-stairs when the company began leave-taking; he stood at the foot of the stair, that he might have one more glance at her. As she came down she was an entirely new picture, though none the less charming, in her wraps. And—oh, bliss! —she saw him, and said,—

"See me to the carriage, Phil, and then find papa for me."

How tenderly he handed her down the carpeted stone steps! He had seen pictures of such scenes, and tried to conform his poses with those he recalled. He opened the carriage door. Lucia stepped in, but her train could not follow of its own volition, so Phil had the joy of lifting the rustling mass that had the honor of following the feet of divinity. Then he closed the carriage door regretfully, but a little hand kindly stole through the window as Lucia said,—

"Good-night. Don't forget to send papa out."

"I won't," said Phil. Then he looked back quickly: the door of the house was closed, so he raised the little hand to his lips and kissed it several times in rapid succession. True, the hand was gloved; but Phil's imagination was not.

CHAPTER XI.

DRIFTING FROM MOORINGS.

MASTER Philip Hayn retired from his second evening in New York society with feelings very different from those which his rather heavy heart and head had carried down to Sol Mantring's sloop only a short week before. No one called him "country" or looked curiously at his attire; on the contrary, at least one lady, in a late party that boarded the elevated train on which he was returning to his hotel, regarded him with evident admiration. Not many days before, even this sort of attention would have made him uncomfortable, but the experiences of his evening at Miss Dinon's had impressed him with the probability that he would be to a certain degree an object of admiration, and he was already prepared to accept it as a matter of course,—very much, in fact, as he had been taught to accept whatever else which life seemed sure to bring.

Of one thing he felt sure: Lucia did not regard him unfavorably. Perhaps she did not love him,—he was modest enough to admit that there was no possible reason why she should,—yet she had not attempted to withdraw that little hand—bless it!—when he was covering it with kisses. She had appropriated him, in the loveliest way imaginable, not only once but several times during the evening, showing marked preference for him. Perhaps this was not so great a compliment as at first sight it seemed, for, hold his own face and figure in as low esteem as he might, he nevertheless felt sure that the best-looking young man in Miss Dinon's parlors was plainer and less manly than himself. But if her acceptance of his homage and her selection of him as her cavalier were not enough, there was that jealous look, twice repeated. He informed himself that the look did not become her ; it destroyed the charm of her expression ; it made her appear hard and unnatural : yet he would not lose the memory of it for worlds.

Could it be true, as he had heard while unintentionally a listener, that her father was not rich? Well, he was sorry for him ; yet this, too, was a ground for hope. After what he had heard, it was not impossible to believe that perhaps the father of the country youth, with his thirty or forty thousand dollars' worth of good land, which had been prospected as a possible site for a village of sea-side cottages for rich people, might be no poorer than the father of the city girl. It seemed impossible, as he mentally compared the residences of the two families, yet he had heard more than once that city people as a class seemed always striving to live not only up to their incomes, but as far beyond them as tradesmen and money-lenders would allow.

As to the talk he had heard about Miss Dinon, he resented it, and would not think of it as in the least degree probable. To be sure, he would not believe her thirty-six, though if she were he heartily honored her that she had lived so well as to look far younger than her years. Still, he was not to be bought, even by a handsome and intelligent woman. It was not uncomplimentary, though, that any one should have thought him so attractive to Miss Dinon,—a woman whom he was sure must have had plenty of offers in her day. But should he ever chance to marry rich, what a sweet and perpetual revenge it would be upon people who had looked, and probably talked, as if he were an awkward country youth !

Then came back to him suddenly, in all their blackness, his moody thoughts over the obdurate facts in the case. Prolong his butterfly day as long as his money would allow, he must soon return to his normal condition of a country grub : he must return to the farm, to his well-worn clothes of antique cut and neighborly patches, to the care of horses, cows, pigs, and chickens, take "pot-luck" in the family kitchen instead of carefully selecting his meals from long bills of fare. Instead of attending receptions in handsome houses, he must seek society in church sociables and the hilarious yet very homely parties given by neighboring farmers, and an occasional affair, not much more formal, in the village.

It was awful, but it seemed inevitable, no matter how he tortured his brain in trying to devise an alternative. If he had a little money he might speculate in stocks ; there, at least, he might benefit by his acquaintance with Marge ; but all the money he had would not more than maintain him in New York a fortnight longer, and he had not the heart to ask his father for more. His father !—what could that good, much-abused man be already thinking of him, that no word from the traveller had yet reached Hayn Farm? He would write that very night—or morning, late though it was; and he felt very virtuous as he resolved that none of the discontent that filled him should get into his letter.

It was nearly sunrise when he went to bed. From his window, eight floors from the ground, he could see across the ugly house-tops a rosy flush in the east, and some little clouds were glowing with gold under the blue canopy. Rose, blue, gold,—Lucia's cheeks, her eyes, her hair; he would think only of them, for they were his delight; his misery could wait: it would have its control of him soon enough.

* * * * * * * *

"Margie, Margie, wake up!" whispered Lucia to her slumbering sister, on returning from the Dinon party.

"Oh, dear!" drawled the sleeper; "is it breakfast-time so soon?"

"No, you little goose; but you want to hear all about the party, don't you?"

"To be sure I do," said the sister, with a long yawn and an attempt to sit up. Miss Margie had heard that she was prettier than her elder sister; she knew she was admired, and she was prudently acquiring all possible knowledge of society against her approaching "coming out." "Tell me all about it. Who was there?" continued the drowsy girl, rubbing her eyes, pushing some crinkly hair behind her ears, and adjusting some pillows so that she might sit at ease. Then she put her hands behind her head, and exclaimed, "Why don't you go on? I'm all ears."

Lucia laughed derisively as she pulled an ear small enough, almost, to be a deformity, then tossed wraps and other articles of attire carelessly about, dropped into a low rocker, and said,—

"Only the usual set were there. I danced every dance, of course, and there was plenty of cream and coffee. Agnes and her mother know how to entertain: it's a real pleasure to go to supper there. But I've kept the best to the last. There was one addition to the usual display of young men,—a tall, straight, handsome, manly, awfully stylish fellow, that set all the girls' tongues running. You've seen him, but I'll bet you a pound of candy that you can't guess his name."

"Oh, don't make me guess when I'm not wide awake yet. Who was it?"

"It—was—Philip—Hayn!" said Lucia, so earnestly that she seemed almost tragical.

"Lucia Tramlay!" exclaimed Margie, dropping her chin and staring blankly. "Not that country fellow who used to drive us down to the beach at Haynton?"

"The very same; but he's not a country fellow now. Upon my word, I shouldn't have known him, if I hadn't known he had been invited and would probably come. I was in terror lest he would come dressed as he did to our reception last week, and the girls would get over their admiration of his talk and tease *me* about him. But you never in your life saw so splendid-looking a fellow,—you really didn't. And he was very attentive to me: he had to be; I took possession of him from the first. He doesn't dance, so I couldn't keep him dangling, but I had him to myself wherever men could be most useful. Margie, what *are* you looking so wooden about?"

"The idea!" said Margie, in a far-away voice, as if her thoughts were just starting back from some distant point. "That heavy, sober fellow becoming a city beau! it's like Cinderella and the princess. Do pinch me, so I may be sure I'm not dreaming."

"Margie," whispered Lucia, suddenly seating herself on the bedside, and, instead of the desired pinch, burying her cheek on a pillow close against her sister's shoulder, "after he had put me into the carriage he kissed my hand,—oh, ever so many times."

"Why, Lucia Tramlay! Where was papa?"

"He hadn't come down yet."

"Goodness! What did you say or do?"

"What could I? Before I could think at all, 'twas all over and he was in the house."

"That country boy a flirt!" exclaimed Margie, going off into blankness again.

"He isn't a flirt at all," replied Lucia, sharply. "You ought to have learned, even in the country, that Philip Hayn is in earnest in whatever he says or does."

"Oh, dear!" moaned Margie; "I don't want countrymen making love to my sister."

"I tell you again, Margie, that he's simply a splendid gentleman,—the handsomest and most stylish of all whom Agnes Dinon invited,—and I won't have him abused when he's been so kind to me."

"Lu," said Margie, turning so as to give one of Lucia's shoulders a vigorous shake; "I believe you think Phil Hayn is in love with you!"

"What else can I think?" said Lucia, without moving her head. Her sister looked at her in silence a moment, and replied,—

"A good deal more, you dear little wretch : you can think you're in love with him, and, what is more, you are thinking so this very minute. Confess, now!"

Lucia was silent; she did not move her head, except to press it deeper into the pillow, nor did she change her gaze from the wall on the opposite side of the room : nevertheless, she manifested undoubted signs of guilt. Her sister bent over her, embraced her, covered her cheek with kisses, and called her tender names, some of which had been almost unheard since nursery days. When at last Lucia allowed her eyes to be looked into, her sister took both her hands, looked roguish, and said,—

"Say, Lu, how does it feel to be in love? Is it anything like what novels tell about?"

"Don't ask me," exclaimed Lucia, "or I shall have a fit of crying right away."

"Well, I'll let you off—for a little while, if you'll tell me how it feels to have your hand kissed."

"It feels," said Lucia, meditatively, "as if something rather heavy was pressing upon your glove."

"Ah, you're real mean!" protested the younger girl. "But what will papa and mamma say? And how are you going to get rid of Mr. Marge? I give you warning that you needn't turn him over to me when I come out. I detest him."

"I don't want to get rid of him," said Lucia, becoming suddenly very sober. "Of course I couldn't marry Phil if he were to ask me,—not if he's going to stay poor and live out of the world."

"But you're not going to be perfectly awful, and marry one man while you love another?"

"I'm not going to marry anybody until I'm asked," exclaimed Lucia, springing from the bed, wringing her hands, and pacing the floor; "and nobody has asked me yet; I don't know that anybody ever will. And I'm perfectly miserable; if you say another word to me about it I shall go into hysterics. Nobody ever heard anything but good of Phil Hayn, either here or anywhere else, and if he loves me I'm proud of it, and I'm going to love him back all I like, even if I have to break my heart afterward. He shan't know how I feel, you may rest assured of that. But oh, Margie, it's just too dreadful. Mamma has picked out Mr. Marge for me, —who could love such a stick?—and she'll be perfectly crazy if I marry any one else, unless perhaps it's some one with a great deal more money. I wonder if ever a poor girl was in such a perfectly horrible position?"

Margie did not know, so both girls sought consolation in the ever-healing fount of maidenhood,—a good long cry.

CHAPTER XII.

IRON LOOKS UP.

THE truth of the old saying regarding the reluctance of watched pots to boil is proved as well in business as elsewhere, as Edgar Tramlay and a number of other men in the iron trade had for some time been learning to their sorrow. Few of them were making any money; most of them were losing on interest account, closed mills, or stock on hand that could not find purchasers. To know this was uncomfortable; to know that the remainder of the business world knew it also was worse: there is a sense of humiliation in merely holding one's own for a long period which is infinitely more provoking and depressing to a business-man than an absolute failure or assignment.

How closely every one in Tramlay's business circle watched the iron-market! There was not an industry in the world in the least degree dependent upon iron which they did not also watch closely and deduce apparent probabilities which they exchanged with one another. The proceedings of Congress, the results of elections, the political movements abroad that tended to either peace or war, became interesting solely through their possible influence upon the iron trade. Again and again they were sure that the

active and upward movement was to begin at once;
the opening of a long-closed mill to execute a small
order, even a longer interval than usual between the
closings of mills, was enough to lift up their collective hearts for a while.   Then all would become faint-
hearted again when they realized that they, like
Hosea Biglow's chanticleer, had been

> "Mistakin' moonrise for the break o' day."

But suddenly, through causes that no one had
foreseen, or which all had discounted so often that
they had feared to consider them again, iron began
to look up; some small orders, of a long-absent kind,
began to creep into the market, prices improved a
little as stock depleted, several mills made haste to
open, and prudent dealers, who had been keeping
down expenses for months and years, now began to
talk hopefully of what they expected to do in the
line of private expenditures.

Good news flies fast; the upward tendency of iron
was soon talked of in New York's thousands of down-
town offices, where, to an outside observer, talk seems
the principal industry.   Men in other businesses
that were depressed began to consult iron-men who
had weathered the storms and endured the still more
destructive calms of the long period of depression.
Bankers began to greet iron-men with more cordiality than of late.   Announcements of large orders
for iron given by certain railroads and accepted by
certain mills began to appear on the tapes of the
thousands of stock-indicators throughout the city.

It naturally followed that Mr. Marge, to whom the

aforesaid "tape" seemed the breath of life, began to wonder whether, in the language of Wall Street, he had not a "privilege" upon which he might "realize." If the upward movement of iron was to continue and become general, Tramlay would undoubtedly be among those who would benefit by it. Would the result be immediate, or would Tramlay first have to go into liquidation, after the manner of many merchants who through a long depression keep up an appearance of business which is destroyed by the first opportunity for actual transactions? Marge had long before, for business purposes, made some acquaintances in the bank with which Tramlay did business, but he did not dare to inquire too pointedly about his friend's balance and discounts. Besides, Marge had learned, through the published schedules of liabilities of numerous insolvents, that some business-men have a way of borrowing privately and largely from relatives and friends.

He would risk nothing, at any rate, by a gentle and graceful increase of attention to Lucia. He flattered himself that he was quite competent to avoid direct proposal until such time as might entirely suit him. As for Lucia, she was too fond of the pleasures of the season just about to open to hold him to account were he to offer her some of them. The suggestion that his plans had a mercenary aspect did not escape him, for even a slave of the stock-tape may have considerable conscience and self-respect. He explained to himself that he did not esteem Lucia solely for her possible expectations; she was good, pretty, vivacious, ornamental, quite intelligent—for a girl, and he had an honest tenderness for her as the daughter of a woman he had really loved many years before, and might have won had he not been too deliberate. But his income was not large enough to support the establishment he would want as a married man, so he would have to depend to a certain extent upon his wife, or upon her father. It was solely with this view, he explained to himself, that he had made careful reconnoissances in other directions: if some ladies who would have been acceptable—Miss Agnes Dinon, for instance—had not been able to estimate him rightly as a matrimonial candidate, he was sure that they as well as he had been losers through their lack of perception. As matters now stood, Lucia was his only apparent chance in the circle where he belonged and preferred to remain. His purpose to advance his suit was quickened, within a very few days, by the announcement on the tape that a rolling-mill in which he knew Tramlay was largely interested had received a very large order for railroad-iron and would open at once.

But indications that iron was looking up were not restricted to the business-portion of the city. Tramlay, who, like many another hard-headed business-man, lived solely for his family, had delighted his wife and daughters by announcing that they might have a long run on the continent the next year. And one morning at breakfast he exclaimed,—

"Do any of you know where that young Hayn is stopping? I want him."

"Why, Edgar!" said Mrs. Tramlay.

"What are you going to do to him, papa?" asked

Margie, seeing that Lucia wanted to know but did not seem able to ask.

"I want another clerk," was the reply, "and I believe Hayn is just my man. I can teach him quickly all he needs to know, and I want some one who I am sure hasn't speculation on the brain, nor any other bad habits. That young Hayn commands respect—from me, at any rate : I used to find down in the country that he, like his father, knew better than I what was going on in the world. I believe he'll make a first-rate business-man : I'm willing to try him, at any rate."

Margie stole a glance at Lucia : that young lady was looking at a chicken croquette as intently as if properly to manage such a morsel with a fork required alert watchfulness.

"The idea of a farmer's boy in a New York merchant's counting-room !" exclaimed Mrs. Tramlay.

"You seem to forget, my dear, that nearly all the successful merchants in New York were once country boys, and that all the new men who are making their mark are from everywhere but New York itself."

"If young Hayn is as sensible as you think him, he will probably be wise enough to decline your offer and go back to his father's farm. You yourself used to say that you would rather be in their business than your own."

"Bright woman !" replied Tramlay, with a smile and a nod ; "but I wouldn't have thought so at his age, and I don't believe Hayn will. I can afford to pay him as much as that farm earns in a year,—say

h   10

fifteen hundred dollars; and I don't believe he'll decline that amount of money; 'twill enable him to take care of himself in good bachelor style and save something besides. I'm sure, too, he'd like to remain in the city: country youths always do, after they have a taste of it."

Again Margie glanced at Lucia, but the chicken croquette continued troublesome, and no responsive glance came back.

"He had far better be at home," persisted Mrs. Tramlay, "where the Lord put him in the first place."

"Well," said Tramlay, finishing a cup of coffee, "if the Lord had meant every one to remain where he was born, I don't believe he would have given each person a pair of feet. And what a sin it must be to make railroad-iron, which tempts and aids hundreds of thousands of people to move about!"

"Don't be irreverent, Edgar, and, above all things, try not to be ridiculous," said the lady of the house. "And when you've spoiled this youth and he goes back to home a disappointed man, don't forget that you were warned in time."

"Spoiled? That sort of fellow don't spoil; not if I'm any judge of human nature. Why, if he should take a notion to the iron trade, there's nothing to prevent him becoming a merchant prince some day,—a young Napoleon of steel rails, or angle-iron, or something. Like enough I'll be glad some time to get him to endorse my note."

Once more Margie's eyes sought her sister's, but Lucia seemed to have grown near-sighted over that

chicken croquette, for Margie could see only a tiny
nose-tip under a tangle of yellow hair.

"My capacity for nonsense is lessening as I grow
older," said Mrs. Tramlay. "I'll have to ask you to
excuse me." Then, with the air of an overworked
conservator of dignity, the lady left the dining-room.

"Excuse me, too," said her husband, a moment
later, after looking at his watch. "Conversation is
the thief of time—in the early morning. Good-by,
children."

Margie sprang from her chair and threw her arms
around her father's neck. She was a fairly affectionate daughter, but such exuberance came only
by fits and starts, and it was not the sort of thing
that any father with a well-regulated heart cares to
hurry away from, even when business is looking up.
When finally Tramlay was released, he remarked,—

"I used to have two daughters:—eh, Lu?"

Lucia arose, approached her father softly and with
head down, put her arms around him, and rested
her head on his breast as she had not often done in
late years, except after a conflict and the attendant
reconciliation. Her father gave her a mighty squeeze,
flattened a few crimps and waves that had cost some
effort to produce, and finally said,—

"I *must* be off. Give me a kiss, Lu."

The girl's face did not upturn promptly, so the
merchant assisted it. His hands were strong and
Lucia's neck was slender, yet it took some effort to
force that little head to a kissable pose. When the
father succeeded, he exclaimed,—

"What a splendid complexion October air brings

to a girl who's spent the summer in the country! There; good-by."

Away went Tramlay to his business. The instant he was out of the room Margie snatched Lucie in her arms and the couple waltzed madly about, regardless of the fact that the floor of a New York dining-room has about as little unencumbered area as that of the smallest apartment in a tenement-house.

CHAPTER XIII.

"WHILE YET AFAR OFF."

THINNER and thinner became the roll of bank-notes in Philip Hayn's pocket; nearer and nearer came the day when he must depart from the city,—depart without any hope that he might ever return. The thought was intolerable; but what could be done to banish it? He might again, and several times, make excuses to leave home and come to New York for a day or two, perhaps on Sol Mantring's sloop, and keep up after a fashion the acquaintance he had made, but to remain in the city any length of time, and spend money as he had been doing, was not to be thought of: the money could not be taken from the family purse, or saved in any way that he could devise.

Oh that he might speculate! Oh that the people who had thought of Hayn Farm as a site for a cottage village would make haste to decide and purchase, so the family's property might be in money instead of land,—solid earth, which could not be spent while in its earthy condition. Oh that he might at least find occupation in New York; he would deny himself anything for the sake of replacing himself on the farm by a laborer, who would be fully as useful with two hands as he, if he might

117

remain in the city. Why had he never had the sense to study any business but farming? There were two stores and a factory at Haynton; had he taken employment in either of these, as he had been invited to do, he might have learned something that would be of avail in New York.

But, alas! it was too late. He must go back to the farm,—go away from Lucia. How should he say farewell to her? Could he ask her to accept an occasional letter from him, and to reply? Would the Tramlays want to spend the next summer at Hayn Farm, he wondered? Should they come, and Lucia see him carrying a pail of pea-pods to the pig-sty, or starting off with oil-skins and a big black basket for a day's fishing off shore, would not her pretty lip curl in disdain? Or if the family wanted to go to the beach for a bath, would he come in from the fields in faded cotton shirt and trousers and band-less old straw hat to drive them down?

No; none of these things should occur. The Tram-lays should not again board at Hayn Farm, unless he could manage in some way to be away from home at the time. He would oppose it with all his might. And, yet, what could he say by way of explanation to his parents? There are some things that one cannot explain,—not if one is a young man who has suddenly had his head turned by change of scene.

How he should say farewell to Lucia troubled him a great deal, particularly as the time was approaching rapidly. To tell her of his love would be unmanly, while he was unable to carry love forward to its natural fruition; but, on the other hand, would it

be right for him to take mere friendly leave after
having betrayed himself over her hand at the carriage window? And if her manifestations of jealousy at the Dinon party meant anything more than
mere desire to monopolize his attention, would she
not hate him if he went away without some expression of tenderness?

The longer he cudgelled his wits, the more inactive
they became. He resolved to call at once, and trust
to chance, and perhaps a merciful Providence, to help
him to a proper leave-taking. He wondered if she
would be at home: he had heard her recapitulate
a succession of engagements which seemed to him
to dispose of a week of afternoons and evenings.
He would seek her father, and ask him when Lucia
could be found at home. He acted at once upon the
impulse, but Tramlay was not at his office. As the
time was about noon, Phil strolled to the restaurant
to which the iron-merchant had taken him. Tramlay was not there, so the young man took a seat
and ordered luncheon. Just as it was served, Marge
passed him, without seeing him, and a young man
at a table behind Phil said to his companion,—

"That Marge is a lucky dog. Have you heard that
he's going to marry Tramlay's daughter? She'll be
rich: iron is looking up."

"Is that so?" asked the other. "When did it
come out?"

"I don't know whether it's announced yet," was
the reply, "but one of the fellows at the bank told
me, and I suppose he got it from Marge: he knows
him very well."

Phil's appetite departed at once : it seemed to him his life would accompany it. His mind was in a daze ; his heart was like lead. His feelings reached his face, and, abstracted and stupid though he felt, he could not help seeing that he was attracting attention, so he paid his bill, went out, and hurried along the street. The first distinct impression of which he was conscious was that there need no longer be any doubt about how to say good-by to Lucia ; a formal courteous note would suffice : he would not trust himself to meet her. Could he blame her ? No : he certainly had no claim upon her heart, nor any reason to really believe she had regarded him as more than a pleasant acquaintance. She had let him kiss her hand ; but had not she herself taught him that this was merely an old-time form of salutation? She had the right to marry whom she would ; yet Marge—— The thought of that man—that lazy, listless, cold, dry stick—being bound for life to a merry, sensitive soul like Lucia drove him almost mad.

Well, the blow was a blessing in one way : now he could go back to the farm without any fears or hesitation. Go back ?—yes, he would hasten back : he could not too soon put behind him the city and all its memories. After all, it was not the city he had dreaded to leave ; it was Lucia, and whatever through her seemed necessary. Now that she must be forgotten, all else might go. He would go back to the hotel, pack his clothes,—how he longed for the money they had cost him !—write a line to Lucia, and take the first train for home. Home ! How shamefully he had forgotten it in the past fortnight! Perhaps this disappointment was his punishment: if so, although severe, it was no more than just. Home! Why, he would rejoice to be once more inside his dirty oil-skin fishing-clothes,—to obliterate the city man he had been aping for a fortnight. Heaven had evidently intended him to be a drudge : well, heaven's will should be done.

Thus reasoned the spirit; but the flesh did not rapidly conform to its leader's will. Phil's teeth and lips were twitching ; he felt it was so ; he noticed that people stared at him, just as they did while he was in the restaurant. This at least he could escape, and he would : so he turned into the first side-street, to avoid the throng. Within a moment he feared he was losing his reason, for it seemed to him that people were pursuing him. There certainly was an unusual clatter of hurrying feet behind him, but— pshaw!—it was probably a crowd running to a fire or a fight. The noise increased ; several wild yells arose, and some one shouted, "Stop thief!" Then Phil's heart stopped beating, for a heavy hand fell on his shoulder. He started violently aside, but there was no shaking off the grasp of that heavy hand: he looked wildly around, and into the eyes of his father.

"Bless you, old boy, how—how fast you do walk !" panted the old man. "I was 'way up—on the other side of the road when—when I saw you turnin' down here. Sol Mantring said I wouldn't know you—if I saw you. Why—I knowed you at first sight."

"Wot's he done?" bleated a small boy in front, for the crowd had already surrounded the couple.

"What's who done?" asked the old man, angrily, after he had looked around and seen the crowd. "Why, you tarnal loafers, can't a man run down the road to catch up with his own son without you thinkin' there's somethin' wrong? I've heerd that in New York ev'ry man suspects ev'ry other man of bein' a thief. Git out! go about your business, if you've got any."

The crowd, looking sadly disappointed and disgusted, slowly dispersed, one very red-faced man remarking that the entire proceeding had been "a durned skin."

The father and son walked along until comparatively alone; then the father said,—

"Somethin's wrong, old boy. What is it?"

Phil did not reply.

"Out of money, an' afraid to send me word?"

"No," Phil replied.

"Then it's *her*, eh?"

Phil nodded. His father squeezed his hand, and after a moment continued,—

"Proposed to her, an' been refused?"

"No," said Phil: "another man has proposed, and been accepted."

"Dear! dear!" sighed the old man. "An' she's dead in love with him, I s'pose?"

"I never saw any sign of it," said Phil, his face wrinkling. "I don't see how she can: he's a dry old stick."

"Rich?"

"Um-m—I don't know," said Phil.

"Know him?"

"Yes, a little. Mr. Tramlay says he lives on his income."

"Easy enough for a bachelor to do that in New York," said the old man, "an' still not have much."

They walked in silence a few minutes; then the old man continued,—

"Sure you weren't mistaken, bub?"

"About what?"

"Sure you reely fell in love? Sure you warn't only in a fit of powerful admiration? Lots of young fellers get took in that way an' spend a lifetime bein' sorry for it."

Phil shook his head.

"She's mighty good-lookin'; I know it. I can take in the p'ints of a gal as good as if she was a colt. Good stock in her, too; that father of hern is full of grit an' go, an' her mother's a lady. Still, you might have been kind o' upset, an' not knowed your own mind as well as you might."

"Father," said Phil, "you remember what you've often said about your horse Black Billy?—'There's only one horse in the world, and that's Billy.' Well, for me there's only one girl in the world,—Lucia."

"That's the Hayn blood, all over," said the old man, with a laugh that grated harshly on Phil's ear.

"And I've lost her," Phil continued. "Don't let's talk about her any more. Don't remind me of her."

"Don't remind you?" shouted the old man, stopping short on the sidewalk. "See here, young man," the father continued, shaking his forefinger impressively, "if I was you, an' felt like you, do you know what I'd do?"

"No," said Phil, amazed at this demonstration by a man whom he scarcely ever had seen excited.

"Well, sir, I'd stay right on the ground, an' I'd cut that other feller out, or I'd die a-tryin'. You'll never be good for anythin' if you don't do one thing or t'other."

Phil smiled feebly, and replied, "You don't understand: there are a great many obstacles that I can't explain."

"'There's a lion in the way, says the slothful man: I shall be slain,'" quoted the old man, from the Book which he had accepted as an all-sufficient guide to faith and practice.

"I've made a fool of myself," said Phil, sullenly, "and I want to go home and take my punishment. I want to go by the first train I can get. I've a long list of things I've promised to buy for different people, but I can't endure New York another day."

The old man studied his son's face keenly for a while, as they resumed their walk; then he said, gently,—

"Perhaps it's best that way. Go ahead. Give me your list, an' I'll 'tend to it. I'll take a day or two in New York myself: it's a long time since I had one. Give us the list; and get out."

Phil fumbled in his pockets for the memoranda that he had neglected so long. Then a new fear came to him, and he said,—

"Father, you know about everything, and can do

almost anything you attempt, but don't go to trying to mend this wretched affair of mine : If I——"

"What?" interrupted the old man. "Meddle in a love-scrape? Have I got to be this old to be suspected by my son of bein' an old fool? No, sir; I never did any love-makin' except for myself, an' I'm not goin' to begin now. You go home an' brace up; I reckon you need a mouthful of country air to set your head right."

11*

CHAPTER XIV.

GOING HOME.

PHILIP HAYN accounted it a special mercy of
Providence that the impulse to leave New York
had been so timed that the train which he caught
would land him at Haynton Station after dark. He
did not feel like seeing old acquaintances that day;
he felt that his face was being a persistent, detestable tell-tale, and that he could not train and command it while so busy with his thoughts. If seen
at all, he intended to offer as few suggestions for remark as possible: so, before leaving his hotel, he
divested himself of every visible trace of city raiment, and clothed himself in the Sunday suit which
Haynton had seen often enough to pass without
remark. He could not restore his shorn superfluity
of hair, but he again put on the hat which for a
year had been his best at home. He even went so
far as to leave for his father a new trunk which he
had purchased, putting his own personal property
into the antique carpet-bag—real carpet—which the
old farmer had brought down. Lastly, that he
might not appear in the least like a city youth, he
carried with him two religious weeklies which some
society for the reformation of hotel-boarders had

caused to be placed in his box in the hotel-office, and
he read them quite faithfully on the train.

Reminders of the old life to which he was returning came to him thick and fast when the train got
fairly out of the city. In a field he saw a man
stripping the leaves from standing corn-stalks, and
although the view was what photographers term
"instantaneous," it was long enough to show the
shabby attire, brown face, shocking bad hat, clumsy
boots, and general air of resignation that marked all
farmers in the vicinity of Haynton. Two or three
miles farther along he saw a half-grown boy picking
up stones in a field of thin soil and adding them to
piles which were painfully significant of much similar work in past days.

Down in a marshy pasture beside the railway-
embankment two men were digging a drainage-
ditch : they were too far apart to be company for
each other, and too muddy to be attractive to themselves. Phil at once recalled much work of like
nature he had done, and more that still depended
upon his muscle to make the entire acreage of Hayn
farm available for cultivation. Estimating according to past experience and newly-acquired knowledge, he found that the number of days of work
required, if paid for at the lowest rate of common
laborers in New York, would amount to twice as
much as the value of the land when improved. It was
easy to see why farmers never got rich. Still, the
farm was his natural sphere ; he had been born to it.
Heaven, in arranging his life-career, knew in advance what he was fit for, and his own difference of

opinion would probably be explained away in time by the logic of events which he could not foresee.

In a dusty road near a little station at which the train stopped he saw two farmers' wagons meet, stop, and their owners engage in conversation. Thus would he, the observer, soon be obtaining whatever news he acquired; instead of every morning opening a newspaper recording the previous day's doings throughout the civilized world, he would be restricted to stories of how Joddles's horse, who had cast himself, was getting along with his scraped hip-joint, and when Bragfew thought he might be likely to kill a beef if he could find somebody to take a forequarter which hadn't been spoken for yet, the chances of Nemy Perkins being "churched" for calling Deacon Thewser a sneaking old sheep-thief, and much more information equally entertaining and instructive. Well, why not? What better news would he himself be likely to offer? He was not going to fall into the sin, warning of which had been given by one of the apostles, of esteeming himself more highly than his neighbors: some people in the vicinity of Haynton did not seem much better than fools, but probably none of them had ever been so idiotic as to fall in love with women far above them in social station and consequently far beyond their reach.

Farther and farther the train left the city behind; more and more desolate the country appeared. It was late October; all crops had been harvested, and many trees had shed all their leaves; the only green was that of grass and evergreens, the latter looking

almost funereal under the overcast sky. The train
entered a region of pine-barrens, through openings in
which some sand-dunes could occasionally be seen.
At times when the train stopped the wind brought
up the sound of the surf, pounding the beach not far
away, and the noise was not as cheering as Phil had
often thought it in earlier days.

Then empty seats in the cars became numerous.
All city people who lived out of town had already
left the train, and the few who got on afterward
belonged in the vicinage. Phil had noted the change
as it gradually occurred, and to a well-dressed couple,
the last of their kind, who occupied seats not far in
front of him, his gaze clung as mournfully as a
toper's eye when fixed upon the last drops that his
bottle can give him. Finally they too disappeared,
and their place was taken by a sallow country-
woman in a home-made brown dress and a gray
bonnet trimmed with green ribbons. He tried to
console himself with the thought that the car would
soon be too dark for colors to be annoying, and that
Haynton was but an hour distant. Then the brilliant thought came to him that he might change the
scene. He acted upon it, went into the next car, and
took a seat. The rustic in front of him turned his
head, stared, and drawled,—

"Gret Gosh! Ef it ain't Phil Hayn, then I'm a
clam-shell! Well, I'd never have knowed ye ef
twa'n't for your father's mouth an' chin." Then
the rustic deliberately gathered his feet and knees
into his seat, and twisted his body until his shoulders
were almost squared to the rear of the car, his whole

i

air being that of a man who had suddenly found a job greatly to his liking, and one to which he intended at once to address himself with all his might.

"Been down to York, eh?" the rustic continued, after getting his frame satisfactorily braced.

"Yes."

The rustic looked so steadily, earnestly, hungrily into the face before him that Phil hastily looked through the window. Some men have been impressed by the historic "stony British stare," others have admired the penetrating glance of the typical detective, or the frontiersman "sizing up" a new arrival; but the Briton, the detective, and the frontiersman combined could not equal the stare of the countryman whose tastes tend toward the affairs of his neighbors.

"York's a good deal of a town, I s'pose," the countryman remarked, after some earnest scrutiny.

"Yes."

"Find anythin' to pay the 'xpenses of the trip?" This after another soulful gaze.

"Shouldn't wonder."

"Carpet-bag seems pooty well stuffed," said the tormentor, after having transferred his glance for a moment to the old satchel that occupied half of Phil's seat.

"Mother wanted a few things that she couldn't find at any of our stores," said Phil.

"See anybody ye knowed?" was the next question, after the stare had returned to its principal duty.

"Not much," Phil replied, with a shiver, well

knowing to whom the man alluded. "How did your turnips average on that new ground, Mr. Bloke?"

"Only so-so. Ye put up at old—what the somethin' was his name?—oh, Trammerly—ye stopped with him, I s'pose?"

"Of course not. Mr. Tramlay doesn't take boarders."

"Ort to hev been willin' to take ye in for a few days, though, I should think, considerin'. Didn't he even offer to?"

"No. Why should he?" asked Phil, beginning to lose his temper. "He paid his way while he was here; I paid mine in New York."

"Oh!" drawled the rustic; then he put on a judicial air, and devoted two or three minutes to analyzing Phil's statement and logic. Either accepting both, or mentally noting an exception for future use, he continued,—

"His gal's as pooty as ever, I s'pose?"

"Which one?"

The questioner's gaze changed somewhat; by various complicated twitches he slowly worked the blankness out of his face and replaced it by an attempt at a smile; then he slowly extended a long arm over the back of the seat, and unfolded a massive forefinger, which he thrust violently into the region of Phil's vest-pocket as with a leer he exclaimed,—

"Kee!"

"Don't be a jackass!" exclaimed Phil, frowning angrily at the fellow. Instead of being abashed, the boor seemed highly delighted, and exclaimed, in somewhat the accent of the animal Phil had named,—

"Haw, haw, haw! Give ye the mitten, did she?"

"It'll be time for any girl to give me the mitten when I give her the chance, Mr. Bloke," said Phil, picking up his bag and starting toward another seat.

"Oh, set down; I didn't think ye was the kind o' feller to go an' git mad at an old neighbor that's only showin' a friendly interest in ye," said the man, in tones of reproach. "Set down. Why, I hain't asked ye half what I want to; you've gone an' put a lot of it out of my head, too, by flyin' off of the handle in that way."

"Haynton!" shouted the conductor, as the train stopped with a crash. Phil hastily rose; so did his tormentor, whose face was an absolute agony of appeal as he said,—

"Lemme help ye up to the house with yer bag. I jist remembered that Naomi has been at me for a week to ask your mother somethin' when I druv by. Might ez well do it to-night as any time: then I can give ye a friendly lift."

"I'm not going to walk out home," said Phil, hastily, "if I can ——"

"Well, I'd jest as lieve ride," said the man.

"Two men and a driver and a big bag aren't going to squeeze into a buggy with seats for only two, if I can help it," said Phil.

"Say," whispered the native, confidentially, as the two reached the platform, "I b'lieve I know where I can borry a team as easy as fallin' off of a log. Jest you stand here a minute or two,—all the boys is dyin' to see you,—an' I'll hook up an' be back."

The man disappeared with great rapidity, for a

being of his structural peculiarities. Phil looked
quickly about, dashed across the track and under
some sheltering trees in a small unlighted street, then
he made a détour through the outskirts of the little
village to reach, without being observed, the road to
his father's farm. The sound of an approaching
wagon caused him to hide quickly behind a clump
of wild blackberries; but when he saw the driver
was not his persecutor he again took the road, mutter-
ing, as he plodded along,—

"Bloke isn't half through with me yet: he said so
himself. And he is only one of fifty or sixty men a
good deal like him,—to say nothing of women ! 'My
punishment is greater than I can bear.'"

Thanks to the charity of deep twilight, there was
nothing unsightly about the familiar road, and as
Phil neared the mass of shadow from which two
lights gleamed just as they had done nightly ever
since he had first approached his home after dark,
his heart gave a mighty bound. Then his heart re-
proached him that he had thought so little about his
mother during his absence that he had not brought
her even the simplest present. He would write back
to his father to get him something which he knew
would please her ; and in the mean time he would
try to give her more love than ever before. If he
could not have a certain new occupant for his heart,
he would at least be as much as possible to those
whom the Lord had given him.

Once within the gate, his better self took entire
possession of him. Neither his mother nor his
brothers should find him other than he had ever

been,—affectionate, cheerful, and attentive. He stole softly to a window of the sitting-room, to see if the family were alone. He saw his two little brothers absorbed in a game of checkers. His mother sat by the table, reading a letter which Phil recognized by the hotel's printed heading; it was his only letter home, written so many days ago that it must have been received long before that evening. Evidently she was re-reading it,—the dear soul!—as people will sometimes do with letters which contain too little, as well as those which are full.

Phil had to keep back some tears of remorse as he sprang upon the veranda and threw the door open. Down dropped the letter, over went the checker table and board, two chairs, and one small boy, and in a moment several country-people were as happy as if the sea had given up its dead or a long-time wanderer had returned. There are some glorious compensations for being simple-minded.

CHAPTER XV.

THE FATTED CALF,—BUT THE NEIGHBORS, TOO.

A THOUGHTFUL man once remarked that a special proof of divine wisdom was that the dear old story of the Prodigal Son did not reproduce any of the conversation of the neighbors with or regarding the naughty boy, for had this also been given as it really occurred, no subsequent penitent would ever have dared to follow the amateur swineherd's example.

Philip Hayn was not a prodigal; he had spent none of his inheritance except as specially ordered by his father, and his only ground of self-reproach was regarding an affair about which the neighbors had no means of obtaining information; yet the special efforts made by the family to manifest their joy at regaining him were unequal to the task of overcoming the disquieting effects of the neighbors' tongues. The dreadful man who had caught Phil on the train had spread the news of the boy's return, so next morning the road from the village to Hayn Farm presented an appearance as animated as if an auction had been announced in that vicinity, or as if some one had been found dead in the woods. Men old and young, wives and maidens, and even little children, devised excuses for visiting the farm. People who came from the other direction were al-

ready supplied with the standard excuse,—they
wanted to borrow something; those who had really
borrowed so often as to doubt their welcome made
heroic efforts to return what they had already borrowed.

To escape the succession of visitors at the house,
Phil went to the barn-yard to see a new family of
pigs of which his little brothers had informed him,
but just above the fence-line he saw two pairs of eyes
—with their attendant heads, of course—that had
been lying in wait for an hour or two, after the
manner of that class of countrymen, evidently
among the last offshoots from the brutes, who apparently have an inherited animal apprehension of
harm should they enter the den of any species higher
than their own.

"Guess you didn't see any pigs like them down to
York?" shouted the owner of one pair of eyes, while
the other pair opened as if they would engulf the
returned traveller. Phil nodded his head negatively
and precipitately retreated to the barn, where he
found quite a respectable old farmer studying the
beach-wagon.

"Reuben reckoned mebbe he could gimme a bargain if I'd take this off his hands," he said, by way
of explanation, "so I thought I'd take a look at it."
The old man shook the wheels, tapped the bed, examined the iron-work closely, remarking, as he did
so,—

"Reckon, by his wantin' to dispose of it, that them
city folks ain't a-comin' here next summer to be druv
down to the beach,—eh?"

" I don't know," said the unhappy youth. He was
grateful to the old fellow for not looking him in the
eye, liké a witness-teaser, as he asked the question,
yet he longed to kick him out of the barn and lock
the doors, so that there would be one less place for
the enemy to lie in wait. He returned to the house,
and entered the kitchen just in time to hear a feminine neighbor say,—

" I s'pose he'll wear his new clothes—them that
Sol Mantring fetched word about—to church on
Sunday?"

Phil abruptly got an axe and went to the wood-lot ;
his first impulse was to take his gun, but half in jest
and half in earnest he told himself that he would
not dare to have arms in his hands if the torment
was to continue. Yet even while in the depths of
the ancestral forest he was not safe, for, on the hollow
pretence of tracking a dog who had been stealing
sheep, a neighbor followed Phil to the woods, found
him by the tell-tale blows of the axe, and had him
at his mercy for a full hour : the visitor had mentally
set apart a half-day for the work.

"There's one way o' gettin' rid of this raft o'
people," said Mrs. Hayn, who rapidly became as indignant as her son at the persistency with which
people brought Lucia's name into conversation.
"One would s'pose that the world had got back to
the way it was in old Father Adam's day, as far as
gals was concerned, an' there was only one female
that anybody could take a notion to. They come
a-pesterin' the life out o' me, just as if I knowed any
more about it than they do,—which I don't." Then

the anxious mother looked slyly, and somewhat re-
proachfully, at her son, who flushed and said,—

"Tell us the way of getting out of it, mother, and
at least one of your children will arise and call you
blessed."

"Why, it's to have the minister an' his wife to tea.
It's manners, an' pretty much everybody knows it,
not to disturb anybody the day they're goin' to have
the minister."

"Let's have him," said Phil, eagerly; "I'll do
anything to help you get ready,—beat eggs, stone
raisins,—anything but go to the store for nutmegs
and be caught by the proprietor and all his customers.
Say, mother, why can't you invite the other min-
isters too, on successive days?"

"You *will* wear your new clothes, though, when
the minister comes, won't you?" asked the old lady,
with some timidity. "You know I hain't seen 'em
on you yet, an' I'm a-dyin' to, though I hain't liked
to put you to the trouble of dressin' up on purpose,
knowin' how men hate to try things on."

Phil promised: he could not resist his mother's
appealing eyes. As the old lady prophesied, the
family were not annoyed the day of the supper to
the minister. Phil's conscience was not easy in
anticipation of the expected guest, for he knew he
would be questioned about the appearance of noted
New York divines whom he would be supposed to
have heard, whereas the only service he had attended
was at the Tramlays' church, the pastor of which
had no notoriety at all. Perhaps it was to punish
his youthful parishioner for neglect of religious privi-

leges that the good man questioned Phil quite closely
about the Tramlay family and delivered a thoughtful analysis of the character of the oldest daughter,
with comments upon the probable effects of marriage
on various qualities of her nature. After each statement he appealed to Phil for corroboration, and on
his way home confided to his wife that he believed
he had fully prepared the dear young brother for
what he might expect should he take the important
step upon which in all probability he was resolved.

Phil endured with becoming fortitude the minister's remarks about Lucia, and the whispered but
not unheard comments of the minister's wife on the
"store clothes," which had been worn in deference
to Mrs. Hayn's request. He ate the three kinds of
solid cake without which no supper to a Haynton
minister was supposed to be complete. He made
unusual effort, his father being away, to cause the
visit one to be pleasantly remembered by the good
pastor. He was rewarded by discovering that his
trip to the city which he had heard called the
"Modern Sodom" and the "American Babylon"
had not destroyed nor even weakened his interest in
religious subjects, and he was prepared to retire with
a more peaceable mind than he had known in several days. But after the table had been cleared and
the uneaten pieces of cake carefully put in an earthen
jar against the next Sunday's tea, and Phil was about
to go to his room, his mother said,—

"Dearie, I s'pose you'll wear your new black things
to meetin' Sunday mornin', won't you?"

"Oh, mother," said Phil, with a frown quickly

c

succeeded by a laugh, "nobody ever wears such a coat to church. Everybody would laugh at me."

"Dear me!" said the old lady, evidently disappointed quite deeply. "I want to know! Then when *be* you goin' to wear it?"

"Never, I suppose," said Phil, his smile vanishing. "I was an extravagant fool to buy that coat. I'll never forgive myself for it."

"Never?" the old lady had echoed. "Then your poor old mother, who loves you better than anybody in the world, is never to see you in it?"

"She shan't wait another hour!" said Phil, hurrying out of the room, and telling himself that his mother cared more for him than all his New York friends combined. He dressed himself anew, with as much care, though not as much trepidation, as when preparing for the Dinon party; he even slipped out of doors and by lighting two or three matches selected a bud from a rose-bush which was carefully covered from the frost every night. He dressed his hair carefully, caressed his moustache into the form a barber had told him was most becoming to his style of face, and squeezed his feet into the low, tight, patent-leather shoes which a shoemaker had assured him were the only proper thing for evening dress. Then he came down-stairs, whistling "Hail to the chief."

Mrs. Hayn hastily adjusted the spectacles she had been polishing, and as Phil entered the room she threw up both hands in amazement and delight. It was worth the price of a coat, thought Phil to himself, to enable that dear, honest old face to express so much enjoyment. As his mother gazed at him, Phil went through the various poses which had been demanded of him when he was a child—even later—and clothes were being fitted to him by the trustworthy Sarah Tweege; he turned around, presented one side view and the other, walked across the room and back, and saluted his mother with his most profound bow. His mother's delight knew no bounds. Finally the good old lady took both his hands, held him at arms' length, looked as if she never could see enough of him; then she gave him a motherly hug, and exclaimed,—

"I should think she'd have fell dead in love with you the minute she clapped her eyes on you, with all those things on."

Phil retired hastily, and when he removed his dress-coat he savagely shook his fist at it.

CHAPTER XVI.

MORE NEWS THAT WAS NOT ENOUGH.

LITTLE by little the excitement over Phil's return abated, being merged in curiosity as to why his father was remaining in the city. Local curiosity was somewhat discouraged, too, by a few sharp retorts to persons who were impertinently inquisitive about the New York developments of Phil's acquaintance with Lucia. There was no lack of stories, however, regarding the couple: in any part of the civilized world, no matter how stolid the inhabitants, there is imagination enough to replace the absent links in a desired chain of facts. All that Haynton and its vicinity really knew about the supposed Hayn-Tramlay affair was that the Tramlays had been at Hayn Farm, that they had a daughter named Lucia whose age did not differ much from Phil's, that Phil had been in New York for more than a fortnight, that he had gone direct from Sol Mantring's sloop to Tramlay's office, that he had been seen in New York in store-clothes, and that he admitted having seen Lucia once or twice. Out of these few facts, which would have been useless to even a detective were he unable to treat them as mere clues to be followed carefully, the enterprising

142

people of Haynton constructed a number of stories, each of which hung together admirably. That they differed radically from one another was not the fault of the local romancers ; they had honestly done their best with the material at hand.

Phil did not regard the matter in this light. When day by day his little brothers returned from school with tales they had heard from class-mates and wondered greatly that they had not first heard them at home, Phil's temper broke loose so suddenly that the boys almost feared to repeat all they had heard. The wrathful young man learned that he had proposed to Lucia and been refused, that he had been accepted, apparently at the same interview, that Tramlay was to build a handsome house on the water front of Hayn Farm for his daughter as a wedding-present, that Phil took his refusal so seriously to heart that he was going to study for the ministry, and that while in New York he had fallen into drinking-habits so deeply that Tramlay had been obliged to write Farmer Hayn to hurry to the city and remove his unfortunate son from the scene of temptation.

Phil grumbled and stormed ; he even vowed that if gossip about him did not end he would go to sea. He thought seriously of publishing a list of denials in the weekly paper, edited in the county town, which devoted a column or two to Haynton news. Then he wondered whether he might not make a confidant of the minister and beg that a sermon be preached on the sinfulness of gossip ; but this plan disappeared abruptly when the statement of his

approaching marriage was traced, almost with certainty, to the minister himself.

But the worst trial of all remained. On Sunday
he met at church and in the Young People's Bible-
Class all the girls who lived at or near Haynton.
Some of them belonged to churches other than that
which included the Hayn family among its members, but for once they waived denominational pref-
erences and went to the First Church, and not only
to see Phil's new clothes and cane, of which Sol
Mantring had brought such astonishing reports.
They were as good and sweet-hearted, those Haynton
girls, as any of their sex on the face of the earth:
fashions a trifle old, and lack of professional advice
as to how best to enhance their natural charms by
borrowing from art, could not disguise the fact that
some of them were quite pretty. It was not their
fault that Phil's heart had gone elsewhere for a mate,
but that the young man himself was greatly to
blame for such a course was the general opinion
among them, and they would have at least the
consolation of seeing how he had been affected by
a step so unusual among Haynton youth. And
what questions those girls' eyes did ask! There
was no need that they should put any of them
into words; Phil understood them all, with the
result that never before on Sunday had he heard
so little of sermon, hymn, or prayer or betrayed
so feeble a grasp of the topic of the day in the Bible-
class.

So seriously was his mind disturbed that he held
himself sharply to account, "examined his evi-

dences" in the time-honored and orthodox manner,
and resolved that lack of occupation was at the bottom of his trouble. He would begin bright and
early Monday morning an extension of the big
ditch in the marsh land : if the mud and stones and
roots and quicksands, the tugging and straining and
perspiring, sure to be incident to the work, would
not cure him, he grimly told himself, then his case
was hopeless indeed.

Bravely he kept his word. At sunrise he was
already on his way to the marsh, and by the middle
of the morning a single sensation encompassed his
entire mind : it was that ditching was the hardest,
dirtiest, forlornest work that ever fell to a farmer's
lot. He dragged one heavily-booted foot after the
other from the ooze, leaned on his spade, and offered
himself five minutes' rest. He looked wearily along
the prolongation of the line of the ditch already
completed, and wondered how many hundred days
the entire improvement would require. Before he decided, his calculations were disturbed by the sound
of the family dinner-bell. He looked at the sun,
which was his only timepiece while at work, and
wondered what could have befallen the hitherto
faithful family clock. Again the bell sounded, and
when he looked in the direction of the house he
saw, on the brow of the hill behind the orchard,
his mother waving her apron to him. Something
was the matter : what could it be? a tramp?—a persistent lightning-rod man? He hurried toward the
house, and soon saw that his mother was waving
also something that looked like a handkerchief and

then like a piece of paper. A little nearer, and he heard his mother shouting,—

"Father's writ! We've got a letter!"

Phil ran nearly all the way up the hill; he had not performed that difficult feat since he and another boy had raced up, in coasting-time, in wild strife as to which should capture a popular girl and take her down on his sled. A letter from his father was indeed an unusual event, for the old man had not been away from home before, except when on jury-duty in the county town, in many years, yet from the old lady's manner it seemed the letter must contain something unusual. As he reached the hilltop his mother placed the sheet in his hand, saying,—

"I thought mebbe you'd better see it at once."

Phil took it, and read aloud as follows:

"DEAR OLD GIRL:

"Your husband is about as usual, though the well-water in this town ain't fit for decent cattle to drink. I've seen some of the sights, and wished more than once that I had you along: if things turn out as they look, though, I'll bring you down in style yet. I've run against the folks that looked at our south ridge with a view to making a cottage village, and, as luck would have it, they knew Mr. Tramlay, who's rolled up his sleeves and done his best to help clinch things and make a good thing out of it for me. I need Phil; Mr. Tramlay wants him too; and I wish you'd tell him to pack his bag and get back here as soon as he can. The boys can take care of the animals, and there's nothing else on the farm but can wait till I get back.

"The Lord be with you all, so no more at present, from

"Your loving husband,
"REUBEN."

"P.S.—That gal ain't no more engaged than I am."

Phil took off his hat, rubbed his eyes, looked away in the direction of the ditch-extension, and made a face at the faithful old spade.

"I s'pose you'd better be thinkin' about gettin' off at once," said his mother.

"Father's will is law," said Phil, in the calmest tone he could command. "Do you think the boys and Carlo can help you take care of the place for a few days?"

"To be sure," said his mother, "an' a powerful sight o' days besides, if it's goin' to save your father from drudgin' away the rest of his days. An' I ain't above sayin' that I'd stand a good deal of loneliness if I thought 'twould end in my stoppin' trottin' around in a pint-pot day in an' day out. An' you," said the old lady, looking at her son, "I want to see the time come when I can take them old boots out to a brush-heap and burn 'em out o' sight an' knowledge. But what does your father mean about that gal not bein' engaged? Is it that Tramlay gal?"

"I suppose so," said Phil, carelessly, though his manner was the result of prodigious effort. "When he found me he asked me about her, along with the other folks, and I told him, just as I'd heard, that she was engaged to be married. Father must have been asking some pointed questions about her. It does beat everything, the interest that old men sometimes take in young women who aren't kith nor kin to them, doesn't it? I guess it's about as well that I'm going back, if only to keep the old gentleman's country curiosity within proper bounds. Don't you think so?"

"She ain't engaged," said Mrs. Hayn, ignoring her son's explanation and his attempt at joking. "She ain't engaged," the old lady repeated; "so you——"

The sentence was not completed, but Phil's face flushed as he looked down at his muddy boots. For the first time since his return he had heard an allusion to Lucia which did not make him uncomfortable.

Within two hours Haynton was shaken from centre—the railway-station—to circumference by the announcement that Phil Hayn, in his store-clothes, had bought a ticket for New York and was already well on his journey. Meanwhile, at Hayn Farm an old woman as deeply interested as any one in the business and other possibilities that had been foreshadowed was doing all in her power to further them: she was spending the afternoon on her knees at her bedside.

CHAPTER XVII.

FATHER AND SON.

YOUTH has some advantages peculiarly its own in the general battle for fame and fortune and in capacity for enjoyment, but for discovering all that may be pleasing in whatever is nearest at hand it is left far behind by age. The school-girl does not care for dainty flavors unless they have candy for a basis ; her mother, with a palate which has been in training for half a century, will get truer enjoyment out of a neighbor's loaf of home-made cake than the girl can find in a shop-full of bonbons. A boy will ramble through an orchard in search of the tree which is fullest and has the largest fruit ; his father, in late autumn, will find higher flavor, and more of it, in the late windfalls which his stick discovers among the dead leaves.

Farmer Hayn was old and weary ; he was alone in his rambles about the metropolis, and he kept close guard on his pocket-book ; but no country youth who ever hurried to the city to squander his patrimony could have had so good a time. He saw everything that the local guide-books called attention to, and so much else which was interesting that Tramlay, whom he had occasion to see for a few minutes each day, said one morning at the breakfast-table,—

"I wish, my dear, that I could steal a week or two from business, so that you and I could poke about New York, personally conducted by that old farmer."

"Edgar!" exclaimed Mrs. Tramlay, "I sometimes fear that old age is taking sudden possession of you, you get such queer notions. The idea of New York people seeing their own city with a countryman for a guide!"

"There's nothing queer about facts, my dear," replied Tramlay, "except that they may be right under our eyes for years without being seen. A few years ago you and I spent nearly a thousand dollars in visiting some European battle-fields. To-day that old fellow has carefully done the Revolutionary battle-fields of New York and Brooklyn, at a total expense of a quarter of a dollar : even then he had a penny left to give to a beggar."

"I never heard of a battle-field in New York or Brooklyn," said Mrs. Tramlay.

"Nor I," her husband replied ; "at least not in so long a time that I'd forgotten the localities. But that old fellow knows all about them : when I drew him out a little he made me plans of each, with pencil on the back of an envelope, and explained how we lost Long Island and New York, as well as nearly two thousand men, when men were far scarcer than they are now. Here"—the merchant drew a mass of letters from his pocket and extracted from them a scrap of paper,—"here's the way it happened ; let me explain——"

"I'm not interested in those stupid old times," said Mrs. Tramlay, with a deprecatory wave of her

hand. "I've heard that in those days there wasn't
a house above Wall Street, no Park to drive in, and
parties began before sunset."

"Ah! to be sure," said Tramlay, with a sigh.
"But old Hayn has seen modern New York too: I
was intensely interested in his description of the
work being done in some of the industrial schools,
where hundreds of little street Arabs are coaxed in
by a promise of full stomachs, and taught to be good
for something; the boys learn how to use tools, and
the girls are taught every branch of housekeeping."

"I really don't see," said Mrs. Tramlay, as she
nibbled a roll, "what there is to interest us in the
doings of such people."

"They're the people," said her husband, raising
his voice a little, "who generally supply us with
paupers and criminals, they being untaught at home,
and consequently having to beg or steal for a living.
It is because of such people that we have iron bars
on our dining-room windows and area-door, and
hire a detective whenever we give a party, and put a
chain on our door-mat and pay taxes to build jails
and asylums and——"

"Oh, Edgar," said Mrs. Tramlay, plaintively, "our
minister told us all this in a sermon nearly a year
ago. I'm sure I listened patiently to it then; I don't
think it's very kind of you to go all over it again."

"No, I suppose not," sighed the merchant, hastily
kissing his family good-by and starting for his office.
In a moment he returned, and said,—

"Just a word with you, my dear. It's nothing
about farmers, or battles, or industrial—— Say," he

whispered, as his wife joined him in the hall, " don't you think I'd better have the doctor drop in to see Lucia? I'm afraid she's going to be sick. She's looked poorly for days, and doesn't seem to have any spirit."

" I'm sure she's lively enough when she's out of temper," said Mrs. Tramlay, "which she is nearly all the while. She's snapped at the children until they hate the sight of her, and I can't speak to her without being greeted by a flood of tears. Margie seems the only one who can do anything with her."

" Umph !" muttered the merchant, taking much time to arrange his hat before the mirror of the hat-rack.

Meanwhile, the old farmer and his son were having a long chat in a hotel bedroom.

"So you see how the land lies," said the old man. "Though I never held that part of the farm at over two hundred an acre, the soil bein' thinner than the lower-lyin' land, an' requirin' a good deal more manure to make decent crops, Tramlay says it'll fetch a clean two thousand an acre when it's cut up, if the scheme takes hold as it's likely to. That's why he advised me to retain an interest, instead of sellin' out-an'-out. I'm to get five thousand in cash for the forty acres, an' have a quarter interest in all sales : that means twenty thousand in the end, if things turn out as Tramlay thinks."

" My !" ejaculated Phil, his eyes opening very wide, and going into a brown study. The old man contemplated him for some time with a smile of supreme satisfaction. Finally he said,—

"Makes you feel a little bit as if you was a rich man's son, don't it, old boy?"

"Indeed it does," Phil replied. "But I don't see how I can help you about it."

"Don't, eh? Well, I'll tell you," said the old man, eying his son closely. "That forty acres is about quarter of the farm-land in value, I calculate, counting out the house an' other buildin's. If I was makin' my will, an' dividin' things up among the family, I'd leave just about that much land to you, with an interest in the house, stock, etcetery, when the Lord sees fit to call your mother. So"—here the old man intensified his gaze—"I've arranged to give my quarter interest in the enterprise to you, as your inheritance: that'll make you a director in the comp'ny, with as much say as anybody else. It'll keep you in York a good deal, though."

"Father!" exclaimed Phil.

"An'," continued the old man, dropping his eyes as soon as his son looked at him, and putting on the countenance in which he usually discussed the ordinary affairs of the farm, "as it may need some money for you to keep up proper style with the people whom you'll have to deal with, I propose to put the five thousand in bank here to our joint account, so you can draw whenever you need cash."

The old man began to pare fine shavings from the tooth-pick which he had cherished ever since he left the dining-room, but Phil compelled a suspension of industry for a moment by going over to his father's chair and pressing the gray head to his breast.

"The other principal stockholders," said the old

man, as soon as he was able to resume his whittling, "are Tramlay an' a man named Marge."

"Marge!" Phil echoed.

"You seem to know him," said the farmer, looking up from under his eyebrows.

"I should think so," said Phil, frowning and twitching his lips a great deal. "He's the man——"

"Well?" asked the old man, for Phil had not finished his sentence. There was no reply, so he continued,—

"The man you thought had caught the gal?"

Phil nodded affirmatively.

"Now you see what comes of goin' off at half-cock," said the farmer. "Lost your expenses two ways, to say nothin' of peace o' mind."

"I heard one man telling another it," said Phil, quite humbly : "so what was I to think?"

"If you believe ev'rythin' you hear about men an' women, my boy, you'll be off your course all your life long. Take a good grip on that."

Again Phil went into a brown study, from which he emerged suddenly to say,—

"It's just what you did, when you supposed you learned she wasn't engaged, isn't it? You believed it, and wrote it at once to me."

"Oh, no!" said the old man, with an air of superiority as he put a very sharp point on what remained of the tooth-pick. "Not much. I've learned always to go to head-quarters for information."

"Why, father," Phil exclaimed, excitedly, "you don't mean to say, after what you promised me, that you went—and—and——"

" Poked my nose into other people's business? Not
I. Mr. Tramlay took me home to dinner,—say, what
an outlandish way these city folks have got of not
eatin' dinner till nigh onto bed-time!—an' after the
meal, 'long about the edge o' the evenin', when
Tramlay had gone for some papers to show me, an'
the old lady was out of the room for somethin', I
took 'casion to congratulate the gal on her engagement; that's the proper thing in such cases made an'
purvided, you know. She looked kind o' flabber-
gasted, an' at last she said 'twas the fust she'd heerd
of it. I tried to git out of it by sayin' if it wa'n't true
it ort to be, if young men in York had eyes in their
heads. But it didn't seem to work. She asked how
I heerd of it, an' I had to say that somebody in the
city had told my son about it."

Phil frowned.

"Then," continued the old man, "she bust out
cryin'."

" Oh, dear!" sighed Phil.

" Well," said the old man, "I see somethin' had to
be done, so I put my arms around her———"

" Why, father!" said Phil, in alarm.

"I put my arms around her, an' said that when a
gal was cryin' she ort to have her parents to comfort
her, an', as neither of 'em was present, I hoped she'd
make b'lieve for a minute or two that I was her grandfather. So she took my advice; an' it seemed to do
her a sight o' good."

" What advice did you give her?" asked Phil.

"None,—in words," said the old man. " Wait till
you're my age; then you'll understand."

"I don't see," said Phil, after a moment or two of silence, "that things are much better than they were. Perhaps she's not engaged; but that fellow Marge is hanging about her all the time. From what I've heard people remark, he's been paying attention to her for a year or two. When the family were at our house last summer he was the only man she talked about. I'm pretty sure, too, from what I've seen, that her mother favors him. So, putting everything together, and thinking about it a good deal, as I've had to do in spite of myself since I've been up home, I've made up my mind that it's a foregone conclusion."

"So you're goin' to flop like a stuck pig, an' let it go on, are you? Just because you've thought somethin' you're goin' to do nothin'. If I'd thought that of you I don't b'lieve I'd have brought you down here to be a business-man in the city. A fellow that hain't got the grit to fight for a gal that he wants is likely to make a mighty poor fist of it in fightin' for a fortune. No, sir; you're not goin' to knuckle under while you've got a father to egg you on. I don't say she's in ev'ry way the gal I'd have picked out for you, but any gal that'll live up to the best that's in her is good enough for any man alive. If you care as much for her as you thought you did when I met you in the street that day, that gal is the one for you to tie to, unless she breaks the rope. A man sometimes gets a bad lickin' in a love-fight, an' a powerful big scar besides, but both together don't do him as much harm as backin' out an' playin' coward."

"I'm not a coward, father," protested Phil, and his eyes flashed as if he meant it.

"You don't mean to be, my boy," said the old man, with a pat on his son's shoulder, "but ev'rythin' in this affair is new to you, an' you're in the dark about some things that mebbe look bigger than they are. That sort of thing'll make cowards out of the best of men, if they give in to it: that's the reason I'm crackin' the whip at you."

"I wonder what Mr. Tramlay wants of me," said Phil, a moment later.

"Reckon you'd better go down and find out," the old man replied.

14

CHAPTER XVIII.

THE NEW CLERK.

"Your mother's out, as usual, I suppose," said Mr. Tramlay to his oldest daughter, as he came home in the afternoon and roamed despondently about the house, after the manner of family men in general when their wives are away.

"She isn't back from her ride yet," said Lucia. "You know the usual drive always keeps her out until about six."

"I ought to know it by this time, I suppose," said the merchant, "and I don't begrudge her a moment of it, but somehow the house is never quite the same when she is out of it."

Lucia looked at her father with a little wonder in her face. Then she laughed, not very cheerfully, and said,—

"Father, do you know that you're dreadfully old-fashioned?"

"I suppose so. Maybe it's force of habit."

Lucia still wondered. She loved her mother, in the instinctive, not over-intelligent way of most young people, but really she could not see what there was about the estimable woman that should make her father long to see her every day of the year and search the house for her whenever he returned. She had never heard her father make romantic speeches, such as nice married people sometimes do in novels; and as for her mother, what did she ever talk of to her liege lord but family bills, the servants, the children's faults, and her own ailments? Could it be, she asked herself, that this matter-of-fact couple said anything when alone that was unlike what the whole family heard from them daily at the table and in the sitting-room?

"Why are you looking at me so queerly?" suddenly asked the father. Lucia recovered herself, and said,—

"I was only wondering whether you never got tired of looking for mother as soon as you came home."

"Certainly not," said the merchant.

"Most husbands do, sooner or later," said Lucia.

"Perhaps I will, some day," the father replied; "and I can tell you when it will be."

"Tell," said Lucia.

"I think 'twill be about the day after eternity ends," was the reply. "Not a day sooner. But what do you know about what some husbands do, you little simpleton? And what put the subject into your little head?"

"Oh, I don't know," said Lucia, dropping upon the piano-stool and making some chords and discords. "It came into my mind; that's all."

"Well, I hope that some day you'll find out to your own satisfaction. By the way, I wish you'd get out of that morning gown. My new clerk is coming to dinner."

"Oh, dear! then I'll have dinner sent up to my room, I think. I don't feel a bit well, and it's awful to think of sitting bolt upright in a tight dress for an hour or two." And Lucia whirled from side to side on the piano-stool, and looked forlorn and cross.

"I suppose it would be impossible to dine in a dress that is not tight?" said the father.

"Papa, please don't tease me : I don't feel a bit well; really I don't."

"What is the matter, child?" asked the father, tenderly. "Too much candy?—too few parties?"

"Oh, nothing, that I know of," said the girl, wearily. "I'll feel better when real cold weather comes, I suppose." She played with the piano-keys a moment or two, and continued,—

"So you have a new clerk? I hope he's nice?— not a mere figuring-machine?"

"Quite a fine fellow," said the merchant. "At least, he seems to be."

"Is he—have you given him the place you intended to offer Philip Hayn?"

"Yes."

"The iron business is real good for a young man to get into, isn't it?"

"Indeed it is, since iron has looked up."

"And that stupid fellow might have had the chance if he hadn't gone off home again without even calling to say good-by?"

"Just so."

"Oh, I don't want to see. him," said Lucia, pettishly. "I'm tired of young men."

"What a mercy it is that they don't know it!"

said her father. "They'd all go off and commit suicide, and then merchants couldn't have any clerks at all."

"Now, papa!" said Lucia, with a crash on the lower octaves of keys, followed by a querulous run, with her thumb, over the shorter strings. "Is the new clerk anybody in particular? What is his name?"

"Philip Hayn."

Lucia sprang from the piano-stool and almost strangled her father with her slender arms.

"Gracious, Lu!" exclaimed the merchant. "Your mother's family must have descended from a grizzly bear. But why this excitement?"

"Because you're a dear, thoughtful old man, who's always trying to do good," said Lucia. "If 'tweren't for you that poor young man might never have a chance in the world. I think it's real missionary work to help deserving people who aren't able to help themselves; I know it is; for our minister has said so from the pulpit again and again."

"I'm real glad to learn that my daughter remembers some of the things she hears in church," said the merchant. "So you think young Hayn deserves a chance in the world, eh?"

"I only know what you yourself have said about him," said Lucia, demurely.

"Good girl! always take your father's advice about young men, and you'll not be mistaken in human nature. Which cut of the roast chicken shall I send up to your room?"

"Oh, I'll try to come down, as it's only Phil: maybe I can coax Margie to help me dress."

l   14*

Lucia slipped slowly from the room, but went up the stairs like a whirlwind. The merchant sat down at the piano and made as dreadful a succession of noises as the much afflicted instrument had ever endured. He had to do something.

A quarter of an hour later Lucia floated downstairs in a robe of pale blue, her face as fresh and bright as dawn.

"Sunrise at sunset!" exclaimed her father. "Well, girls are possessed to upset the natural order of things, I suppose. But, my dear daughter, you've put the rouge on too thick; don't you think so?"

"Father!" exclaimed the girl, and the flush of her cheeks spread to her brow.

"Edgar," said Mrs. Tramlay, who came in a moment or two after, "see how foolish you were to think Lucia ill. I never saw her looking better."

"Yes," said the merchant, dryly; "I told her the doctor was coming. That's often enough to cure the ailments of some children, you know." Then the merchant devoted ten minutes of business tact to the task of explaining to his wife the reasons of Philip's return to New York; he also enlarged upon the Haynton Bay Improvement Company, and the probability that if the Tramlays were to build the first and handsomest house on the new property Mrs. Tramlay would naturally be the fashionable leader of whatever section or sub-section of society might select the place as a summer home. Mrs. Tramlay was inclined to be conservative on the subject, but when she learned that Marge was a stockholder and director in the company she became quite cheerful.

Phil was not so happy as he should have been while on his way to the Tramlays'. He wondered how he should be able to greet Lucia without betraying the mixed emotions which he was sure the first sight of her face would cause him. He had a firm conviction that he would feel awkward and act accordingly, and his remembrance of various men whom he had seen behaving awkwardly in the presence of young ladies made him certain that Lucia and Margie would laugh at him when his back was turned. He did not realize that in meeting, as well as in fighting, the burden of action does not all rest upon one person. Neither did he take into consideration the tact which some maidens acquire in a year or two spent in society. As he was ushered into the parlor, with a face which he was sure was sober and set, Lucia approached him with a pleasant smile, and exclaimed, as heartily and unaffectedly as if she were a Haynton girl,—

"How do you do, Phil? I'm ever so glad to see you back again."

Away went all sense of soberness, hesitation, and doubt; the young man's soul leaped to his face, and he held so long the little hand offered him that Lucia, perhaps remembering some impulsive demonstrations toward that graceful member, withdrew it before any attempt to release it had begun. Then the girl began a rapid series of questions about Hayn Farm and its occupants, and Phil made cheery replies, and Tramlay, after gazing at the couple from the back parlor, retired to his library to indulge undisturbed in as much vigorous

and affirmative head-shaking as the situation seemed
to justify.

"How do you think you will like the iron business,
Mr. Hayn?" asked Mrs. Tramlay at dinner.

"Greatly, so far as I know it," Phil replied. "Up
to date my duties have been to go to lunch, read the
morning papers, and chat with a railroad company's
vice-president about off-shore fishing."

"We always try to break in our young men pleasantly," said Tramlay, "so they'll be willing to promise long service for small money: then we begin to
put on heavier chains, one by one."

"Papa's clerks have a hard time, if they happen to
be nice," said Lucia. "They have to get postage-
stamps for Margie and me when we happen in at the
office, and find small change for us when we lose our
pocket-books, and take us out to lunch when we
come down town and don't find papa in, and sometimes they have to come to trains for us when we've
been a few miles out of town on a visit and the team
doesn't get in before dark."

"Then I shall earnestly strive to be nice," said
Phil.

"There's some down-town place," said Margie,
"where papa gets lovely candy a great deal cheaper
than up Broadway; but he forgets it half the time,
so we sometimes have one of the clerks order it sent
to papa's desk,—that is, clerks who know how to
select candy," said Margie.

"My education in that respect," said Phil, "has
not been as thorough as if I could have foreseen such
necessity for it; but I will resume my studies at once."

"Are you a good judge of tea?" asked Lucia. "Mamma has not been quite herself since one of papa's clerks went to Pennsylvania to take charge of a rolling-mill. The good man used to spend hours in the tea-importers' warehouses, down near the office, searching for the kind of tea that mamma dotes on."

"You children are not to worry Phil with any of your trifling affairs," said the head of the house. "I want you all to understand that, besides having a desk in my office, he is a large operator in real estate,—a capitalist,—a sort of monopolist, in fact, for he is secretary and a director of the Haynton Bay Improvement Company, which monopolizes one of the finest bits of shore front on the Atlantic Coast."

"Haynton Bay!" said Lucia, in wonder. "Why, that is where Hayn Farm is."

"Wise child!" said her father; "and that fine bluff portion of the farm that overlooks the bay is the company's property. You'll never again cut your shoes to pieces on the oat stubble on that bluff, for when next you see the place it will be covered by fine villas, the handsomest of which you probably will some day see mentioned in the newspapers as the country-seat of the well-known merchant prince, Edgar Tramlay, Esq., father of the charming——"

"Edgar! Edgar!" said Mrs. Tramlay.

"And, as I was saying," continued Tramlay, "no purchaser's title will be good without the signature and official seal of Mr. Philip Hayn. Candy and postage-stamps, indeed! Why, such a man's time ought to be valued at about a dollar a minute."

Then Phil was rich, Lucia said to herself. She did not much care, and she knew even less, about business-details; a fortune on paper was as good as any other kind, so far as she knew; but what she did very distinctly understand was that no one, not even her mother, would again have occasion to speak of Phil as a poor man, or even a countryman. Some young men who were accounted great catches were only secretaries and even assistant secretaries of one thing or other; she knew it, because she had seen their names in dividend notices and other advertisements in newspapers. How would the change in his fortunes affect her mother, she wondered. Mrs. Tramlay certainly was more affable to the young man than she ever had been before, and after dinner she even took Phil's arm in returning to the parlor: the act signified nothing to Phil, but it set Lucia's little heart dancing gayly. When Phil departed, soon after dinner, to accompany his father, by request, to a meeting of the "Society for the Amelioration of the Spiritual Condition of Savage Tribes," Lucia lost very little time in signalling Margie with her eyes and going up to her room. A moment later Margie bounced in, closed the door, and exclaimed,—

"Lucia Tramlay! I wouldn't have believed it if I hadn't seen it with my own eyes. The idea of mamma, with the blood of a dozen High Dutch and Mayflower families in her veins, taking the arm of a countryman!"

"When there was no call for her to take any one's arm," added Lucia, "the affair being only an every-day family dinner."

"''Twas simply paralyzing," said Margie; "but 'twas a sign that everything will be all right from this time forward. Dear me! I can imagine just how your new visiting-cards will look: 'Mrs. Philip Hayn.'"

"Margie, Margie," said Lucia, in a quick whisper, "do be quiet. I don't even know whether he really loves me."

"That's because you didn't sit at table where you could see his face all the while, as I did. Besides, a stone image would fall in love with you to-night: you never looked so perfectly entrancing in all your life."

So, between all she had seen and heard, Lucia's head was crowded with pleasant dreams long before it pressed its pillow.

CHAPTER XIX.

BETWEEN his duties at the office of the Haynton
Bay Improvement Company and his earnest desire
to master the mysteries of the iron trade, Philip
Hayn found very little time for dropping into moody
reflections. Like many another young man in business, he became convinced that a great deal of telling work might be done outside of business-hours:
so he spent many evenings and occasional days in
endeavoring to forward the interests of his employer,
and of the Improvement Company, in which Mr.
Tramlay was as largely interested as himself.

He had more than business to absorb his thoughts,
for his stock of knowledge regarding human nature
was at first entirely inadequate to the demands
made upon it. At Haynton it was a safe rule that
a man whose appearance and manner were those of
a gentleman could be safely regarded as, at least, an
honest man; in New York he found this assump-
tion caused some of his plans to be utterly shattered
by Tramlay's more experienced hand. The railroad-
men who wanted iron, to be paid for partly by stock
in their roads, he learned to distrust if they were
habitually well dressed and wore kid gloves when
visiting Tramlay's office, but he occasionally saw his

168

employer neglect an appointment, even with his family, and devote his entire time to some insignificant, badly-dressed little fellow, and even to an occasional awkward man who seemed, as he really was, the farmer-secretary and treasurer of a lot of fellow-farmers who had planned a short road for their own benefit. The amount of cash that such a man could pay was seldom large, but not so the probable profit on the stock which Tramlay received "to boot."

A pleasing relief from the work of his two offices was Phil's occasional evenings at Tramlay's home, which he had been so heartily urged to regard as his own that he no longer waited for special invitations. In spite of his pressing duties, he had devoted himself to being "nice," as Lucia had termed the condition which made the family avail themselves of the services of Mr. Tramlay's clerks. He improved upon his instructions so far as always to have in his pockets enough postage-stamps for the girls' letters, and to see that boxes of candies from "the place somewhere down town" reached the house without first lying neglected for a day or two upon his employer's desk. When Margie and Lucia were returning from a short visit out of town, he was at station, wharf, or ferry to meet them, regardless of what railway-magnate from out of town might be already accessible at a hotel, and the pang of hurrying away afterward was always sweetened by the gentle protests that no subsequent conversation could banish from his ear.

And yet, as he informed himself in occasional moments of leisure, the interest that lay closest to

H   15

his heart was not being advanced visibly. Lucia seemed always glad to meet him, always sorry to part with him; but was she not so to all mere acquaintances whose society was not unpleasing? She never made an excuse to cut short his conversation, no matter if he talked on subjects of which she evidently was ignorant; but had he not always been accustomed to patient listeners? She sometimes asked questions that seemed beyond her taste, as the subjects certainly were beyond her ken; but might not ordinary human desire for knowledge prompt any girl to do the same?

Sometimes he would bitterly inform himself that of his host's two daughters any listener might imagine Margie, instead of her sister, the object of his affection. Margie, whose feelings and manner and enthusiasm lacked the restraint which a year or two of society will impose on an observing maiden, was as artless and effusive and affectionate as if Phil were an ideal older brother, if not a lover. Of course Margie was not in love with him; for was she not continually sounding Lucia's praises? To her the world seemed to live and move and have its being solely for Lucia. Phil had never before seen such affection between sisters, and it seemed all the more wonderful as he recalled some frequent passages of words in which the two girls had indulged at Hayn Farm, not a half-year before. Margie seemed to have adopted him as a big brother, and it was quite delightful, as well as a new sensation, he having no sisters of his own, but he did wish that the same spirit—not exactly the same, either—might be manifested by Lucia.

Another disquieting thought came from the frequency with which Marge visited the Tramlay abode. He had heard almost too much of Marge before he ever saw him, but now he saw far more. It seemed that Phil never could visit the Tramlays without either finding Marge already there, or having him come in just as a pleasant *tête-à-tête* with Lucia was fairly under way. That Marge did not approve of the cordiality with which Phil was received was quite evident, in spite of his impassive demeanor, and Phil felt none the easier that Marge showed him many courtesies, and introduced him quite freely among his club acquaintances. Marge explained that many of these gentlemen had money and might be persuaded to purchase cottage-sites of the Haynton Bay Company; but if this was his purpose why did he not conduct the negotiations himself? Occasionally Phil suspected that there were dark designs hidden in Marge's invitations to quiet little games at the club, and his rather sneering replies, to Phil's refusals, that all gentlemen played cards sometimes; still, such games as he chanced to see were not for large sums, nor were they attended by any of the excitement that is supposed to make inexperienced players reckless.

Almost as disturbing was Mrs. Tramlay's manner. At times she was affable and almost hearty in her manner toward Phil; again she was reserved and distant. What did it mean? Did she divine his purpose and resent it? or could it be that she was

impatient that he did not pay his court with more
fervor? Could he have overheard some of the con-
versations of which he was the subject, he would
have been enlightened, yet scarcely more hopeful.

"Edgar," said Mrs. Tramlay to her husband one
evening, "young Hayn comes here so much that no
one else is likely to visit Lucia with any serious intentions."

"Well, why should they?" asked her husband.
"Isn't he good enough for a son-in-law?"

"I'm not even sure that he aspires to that position," said Mrs. Tramlay.

"Aren't you? I'm afraid, then, you'll soon need
to wear glasses, my dear."

"Don't joke about it, please: it's a serious subject."

"Yes," sighed the merchant; "one's first
glasses——"

"You know very well I don't mean glasses," said
the lady, with some petulance. "This is Lucia's
second season, and desirable young men are rare.
'Twould be unfair to her to have a man dawdling
about her, acting frequently as her escort——"

"Assisted by her mother——"

"That doesn't alter the case: it makes it all the
graver in other people's eyes."

"Well, my dear, I see plainly enough that young
Hayn has fixed intentions; and I'm as fully satisfied
that they are entirely to Lu's taste."

"Then the question is, should it be allowed to go
on?"

"Why not, if they love each other, or want to?"

"Because we want our first daughter to make as good a match as possible, and I don't see that the young man's prospects are very brilliant. If the Improvement Company shouldn't succeed, he'll be nothing but your clerk, with no certainty nor any expectations."

"I feel entirely easy about the money I've put into the Improvement Company," said the merchant, "and Phil will do as well as I, he having an equal number of shares. If worst comes to worst with him from that speculation, and he and Lu continue to like each other, I can take him into partnership. That would give him financial standing : there are plenty of young men of good families who would pay well for such an opportunity, for iron is up, and to stay."

Mrs. Tramlay tossed her head, and replied, "I didn't ever suppose it would be necessary to set a young man upon his feet in order to get a husband for one of our daughters."

"Quite right: don't suppose so yet, either, for I assure you he is fully earning whatever it might be necessary to give him. I find that he makes a very favorable impression upon the class of people who visit the iron-houses, or whom the iron-houses look after. He's already got two or three desirable little orders, besides being on the track of others."

"But he's only a clerk, after all," persisted Mrs. Tramlay.

"Say but the word, and I'll make him my partner to-morrow," said Tramlay.

"Don't be hasty," replied the lady, in some alarm. "He is not Lucia's only chance, you know."

15*

Tramlay looked inquiringly; his wife appeared embarrassed, and averted her eyes.

"Oh! You mean Marge, I suppose? Well, if Lu should really want him, I wouldn't like to make her unhappy by saying no. But really, my dear,"—here the merchant put his arm around his wife,—"really, now, don't you think that a man who was a beau of yours a quarter of a century ago is rather mature to be the husband of an impulsive girl?"

"Young wives can't live on impulse alone," said Mrs. Tramlay. "Mr. Marge has means."

"Not to any great extent, that any one has been able to discover," interrupted the merchant.

"And he has social position, which is of more importance in New York than anything else," continued the wife. "He knows many prominent people whom we do not, and if he were to marry Lucia it would improve Margie's opportunities. We haven't gone into society as much as we should, and I'm afraid our daughters will have to suffer for it."

"Don't trouble your head with any such fears," said the husband, with more than his usual earnestness. "Girls like ours—bless them!—aren't going to make bad matches."

"Besides," said Mrs. Tramlay, retracing her thoughts, "Mr. Marge doesn't look the least bit old: he is not the kind of man to grow old. I can't see that he appears a day older than he did years ago."

"Bless your sentimental heart!" said the merchant. "He doesn't, eh? Well, it does you credit to think so, and it doesn't make me jealous in the least."

"If the Company succeeds," continued Mrs. Tramlay, "Mr. Marge will be as much the gainer as you or young Hayn, won't he?"

"Certainly."

"Then he'll be that much better off than this young man you're so fond of?"

"Yes, if he does nothing foolish in the mean time; but I have my doubts of the financial stability of any man who can't pass a stock-ticker without looking at it. Wall Street exists solely for the purpose of absorbing such men's money."

"Mr. Marge is no fool," said Mrs. Tramlay.

"He's no wiser than some veterans who have had to leave their millions in the street and live on their children for ever after."

"The Improvement Company has only about forty acres, I believe you said?"

"Just forty."

"And two thousand an acre is the most you hope for?"

"Yes."

"That would be eighty thousand dollars : four into eighty goes twenty times, and——"

"If I'd known you'd such a head for business I would have asked you to put a housekeeper in charge of the family, so I could have your services at the office," said Tramlay.

"Twenty thousand dollars would be very little for a young man to marry on in New York,—and in our set."

"Twenty thousand, and a salary which I must soon increase in simple justice ; also, expectations from his father's estate in the course of time. I don't remember to have told you, though, that the young man was long-headed enough to suggest that his father should buy options on the continuation of the ridge,—there are several hundred acres in all, distributed among different farms,—and the old fellow has worked it so skilfully that we have the refusal of it all, for a year, at a trifling outlay in money. There's genuine city business capacity in that young man's head,—he?"

"It appears so," Mrs. Tramlay admitted.

This admission might have been of great comfort to Phil could he have heard it, but, as he never received any information, except through his alternating hopes and suspicions, he was obliged to remain in doubt. His principal hope, aside from that based on Lucia's willingness to devote any amount of time to him, was obtained through the manner of the head of the family. Tramlay was communicative as wise merchants usually are to their employees ; he was also confidential : evidently he trusted Phil implicitly, for he told the new clerk all his business expectations and hopes, instructed him carefully regarding every one whom the young man was to see for business-purposes, and threw much important work upon him. It seemed impossible to misconstrue the purpose of all this : at the very least, it implied a high order of respect ; and the respect of a possible father-in-law was not an ally to be underrated. Besides, Tramlay frequently put Lucia in his charge when she was out for an evening ; and this implied a still higher order of trust.

But, after all, the hopes that were strongest and most abiding were formed in the Tramlay parlor, while Lucia was apparently only acting the part of a listener. The young man occasionally found himself expressing his own opinion freely, and to great extent, on subjects that interested him, and the flow of language was interrupted only by badly-concealed yawns from Mrs. Tramlay and Margie. Where to them could be the interest in the latest campaign against the Indians, or methods of ventilating school-rooms, or the supposed moral purpose underlying England's continued occupation of Egypt? Such questions were fit only for men, thought Mrs. Tramlay and her second daughter: the mother sometimes said, after excusing herself from impromptu lectures on these or kindred topics, that the young man from the country loved to hear himself talk, and Margie half believed that Phil only began what she denominated " harangues" in order to clear the room, so that he might have Lucia to himself.

But to all that Phil said, no matter how heavy the subject, Lucia listened patiently, attentively, and often with an air of interest. Sometimes she attained sufficient grasp of a statement to reconstruct it, in words, though not in facts, and return it to the original maker, who, in the blindness of bliss, immediately attributed it to Lucia's mental superiority to the remainder of the family. Had he seen her afterward perplexedly pinching her brow as she appealed to cyclopædia or dictionary to make his meaning clearer, he might have revised his opinion as to her intellect, yet he would have been the surer of what to him, just then, was more desirable than the collective intellect of the world.

m

CHAPTER XX.

MR. MARGE had breathed a gentle sigh of relief when he heard of Philip Hayn's sudden departure from the metropolis : had he known the cause of the young man's exit he would in gratitude have given a fine dinner to the male gossip who had said in Phil's hearing that Marge was to marry Lucia. Not knowing of this rumor, he called at the Tramlay abode, ostensibly to invite Lucia and her mother to the theatre, and from the manner of the ladies he assumed that Phil, with the over-confidence of youth, had proposed and been rejected. Marge's curiosity as to what the head of the family could want of the young man was allayed by Mrs. Tramlay's statement that the visit was due wholly to her husband's ridiculous manner of inviting each country acquaintance to come and see him if he ever reached New York ; his subsequent hospitality to Philip was only for the purpose of keeping on good terms with some old-fashioned people who might some day again be useful as hosts, and who could not be managed exactly as professional keepers of boarding-houses.

But Marge's curiosity was rearoused the very day after he received this quieting information, for he

178

chanced to meet the merchant with the young man's
father, and was introduced to the latter.

"Instantly the old question returned to his lips,
"What can Tramlay want of that fellow?" Again
his curiosity subsided, when he learned of the cot-
tage-city project, and, while agreeing to assume a
quarter of the expense of the enterprise, he complimented Tramlay on his ability to find something
to profit by, even while ostensibly enjoying an occasional day's rest in the country. But when, a day
or two later, Phil reappeared and was presented to
him as the old farmer's representative,—as the real
holder, in fact, of a full quarter of the company's
stock,—Marge looked suspiciously at the merchant,
and asked himself,—

"What can Tramlay want of that fellow?"

Reasoning according to the principles on which
many small real-estate companies or corporations de-
veloping a patent are formed, Marge soon informed
himself that Tramlay, whose shrewdness he had
always held in high respect, preferred the son to
the father, as being the easier victim of the two.
The processes of frightening out or "freezing out"
an inventor or farmer who had put his property in
the hands of a stock company were not entirely
unknown to Marge, and he naturally assumed that
they would be easier of application to a green young
man like Philip than to a clear-headed old man, as
farmer Hayn seemed to be. But if the rural element
of the company was to be despoiled of its own, Marge
proposed to see that not all the spoils should go to
the merchant. How better could he improve his own

position with Tramlay than by making himself the
merchant's superior in finesse? He would have the
advantage of being able to watch Phil closely, and
of knowing first when he might be inclined to sell
out at a sacrifice : should the young man, like most
of his age and extraction, develop an insatiable appetite for city joys that cost money, he, Marge, would
cheerfully supply him with money from time to time,
taking his stock as security, and some day the merchant would suddenly find himself beaten at his
own game. The mere thought of such a triumph
impelled the deliberate Marge to take a small bottle
of champagne with his mid-day luncheon,—a luxury
which he usually reserved until evening, at the club.

But again he was startled when a light-headed
friend complained that, although the said friend's
father had been promised a place for his son in
Tramlay's office when the iron trade should look
up, Tramlay had taken in a countryman instead.
His own eyes soon confirmed the intelligence, and,
as Tramlay made no explanation or even mention
of the fact, Marge again found himself asking,—

"What can Tramlay want of that fellow?"

Evidently it meant either business or Lucia. Perhaps the merchant during the long depression of the
iron trade had borrowed money of the young man's
father, or was now borrowing of him, to avail himself of his increasing opportunities. (Marge had the
city man's customary but erroneous impression as to
the bank-surplus of the average "well-to-do" farmer.)
If Tramlay were merely a borrower, except against
notes and bills receivable, iron had not looked up

enough to justify a prudent man in becoming the
merchant's son-in-law. If there had been such
transactions, perhaps a share of the business was
to pay for them. Inquiries of his banking-acquaint-
ances did not make the matter clearer to Marge; so
he resolved to devote himself to the new clerk, as
he could safely do in his capacity of co-director of
the Improvement Company. The young man had
considerable self-possession, Marge admitted to himself; but what would it avail against the fine methods
of a man of twice his years, all spent among men
who considered it legitimate business to pry into the
business-affairs of others?

So Marge began operations at once; no time was
to be lost. He had no difficulty in making his ap-
proaches, and his courtesies were so deftly offered
that Phil could not help accepting many of them
and feeling grateful for kindness rendered. The
young man's suspicions were soon disarmed, for, like
honorable natures in general, he abhorred suspicion.
That there was a purpose in all of Marge's actions
Phil could not avoid believing, but little by little he
reached the conclusion that it was simply to forward
the Improvement Company's prospects. As Marge
himself said, Phil knew the company's land thoroughly, and was the only person who could talk of it
intelligently. Any vestiges of distrust that remained
were swept away when Marge succeeded in having
the privileges of his club extended to Phil for three
months, pending application for admission. It was
a small club, and exclusive; Phil heard it named
almost reverently by some young men who longed

16

to pass its portals, and among its members were a few men of a social set more prominent than that in which the Tramlays moved.

To Marge's delight, Phil began to spend money freely at the club : Marge had seen other young men do likewise, and there was but one end to be expected if their parents are not rich. Phil drank no wine, smoked no cigars, yet when he thought it proper to give a little dinner the best that the club's caterer could supply was on the table. He did not seem to have any other expensive habits, except that he dressed so carefully that his tailor's bill must be large ; still, a man who gives dinners at clubs must have plenty of money. From being a source of gratification, Phil's free use of money began gradually to cause Marge dismay. Where did it all come from ? He could scarcely be earning it in his capacity of junior clerk in an iron-house. Could it be that Tramlay had him in training for the position of son-in-law, and was paying the cost of introducing him favorably to the notice of some sets of New York society to whom he could not present him at his own house ? Such a course would be quite judicious in a father desiring wider acquaintance for his daughter when she should become a bride ; but, if it really were being pursued, would he, Marge, ever hear the end of the rallying to which his own part in the programme would subject him ?

There was more torment in this view of the case than Marge had ever experienced in his life before, and it robbed him at times of his habitual expression to an extent that was noticeable and made him the

subject of some club chat. No matter how exclusive
a club may be, no matter how careful in the selection
of its members that none but gentlemen may be upon
its list, it cannot prevent a small, gradual, but distinct and persistent aggregation of gossips,—fellows
whose energies, such as they are, tend solely to investigation of the affairs of their acquaintances. There
was not an hour of the day or night when several of
these fellows could not be found at Marge's club,
lounging as listlessly and inconspicuously as so many
incurables at a hospital, but Marge knew by experience that these were the only fellows worth going to
if he wanted to know all that was being said about
a member, particularly if it was uncomplimentary.
And now, confound them, possibly they were talking
about him, and intimating that he was being used to
improve the standing of his own rival!

Still, as he informed himself, all his annoyance
came from a mere supposition, which might be entirely without foundation. Perhaps the young man
had means of his own; he had not looked like it
when he first appeared in New York, but appearances
sometimes were deceitful. Marge had heard Tramlay
allude to Phil's father as an honest old farmer to
whom fortune had not been any too generous; but
perhaps he had been estimating the old man's possessions only by New York standards: was it not
the farming-class that originally took up the greater
part of the government's great issues of bonds?

And, yet, if the young man had money of his own
or of his father's, where did he keep it? Had he
ever displayed a check, to indicate his banking-place,

Marge would have found ways of ascertaining the size and nature of his account. But, though he had several times seen Phil pay bills which were rather large, the settlements were always made with currency. Was it possible, Marge asked himself, that the traditional old stocking was still the favorite bank of deposit for the rural community? It might have relieved his mind to know that the countryman's customary method, when he has money, is to carry a great deal of currency, and that instead of making payments by check he draws bank-notes with which to pay.

And so the weeks went on, and Marge did not accomplish anything that he had intended when he began to devote himself to the young man from the country. Phil borrowed no money, squandered none at cards, did not run into dissipation, offered no confidences, and, although entirely approachable, was as secretive about his personal affairs as if he had been sworn to silence. Even on the subject of Lucia, which Marge had cautiously approached several times, he talked with a calmness that made Marge doubt the evidence of his own senses. Phil did not even wince when Marge reminded him of the horse he knew of that would match Marge's own, the reason assigned being that the sleighing-season was coming and he would be likely to frequently take the ladies of the Tramlay family out behind two horses. On the contrary, Phil had the horse found and sent to New York at his own expense, saying he could make himself even by selling, in case the animal did not please Marge.

The horse arrived; he pleased Marge, who was delighted with the impression the new team made upon the family and his acquaintances generally, Phil included. Marge was not equally pleased, however, when within a few days farmer Hayn sent his son a pair of black horses which, though of no blood in particular, had a quality of spirit and style not to be expected of high-born animals long accustomed to city pavements and restricted to the funereal gait prescribed by Park Commissioners' regulations. With their equally untamed country-bred owner to drive them, the span created quite a sensation, and, to Marge's disgust, the Tramlays seemed to prefer them to the pair on which he had incurred extra expense for the sake of Lucia and her mother.

His plans foiled, his wonderings unanswered, his direct questions evaded, his enemy persisting in acting only as a friend might act, and the father of his intended avoiding mention of Phil so carefully as to excite suspicion, yet inviting Marge to his house as freely as ever, the man of the world was unable to reach any fixed decision, and was obliged again and again to repeat to himself the question,—

"What can Tramlay want of that fellow?"

16*

CHAPTER XXI.

HAYNTON ROUSES ITSELF.

ONE of the blissful possessions of the man of mature years is the self-control which spares its possessor the necessity of consuming time and vitality in profitless excitement. Farmer Hayn, returning to his native village, had a great deal more on his mind than Phil when that youth preceded him a few days before. It is true that Phil was bemoaning what he believed to be the loss of a sweetheart, but the old man's thoughts were equally full of the possible gain of a daughter,— an earthly possession he had longed for through many years but been denied. He had also a large and promising land-speculation to engage his thoughts,—a speculation which, apparently, would bring the family more gain in a year than three generations of Hayns had accumulated in a century. He was planning more enjoyments for his gray-haired, somewhat wrinkled old wife, should the Improvement Company's plans succeed, than any happy youth ever devised for his bride, and he knew exactly how they would affect the good woman,—a privilege which is frequently denied the newly-made husband.

And yet his mind and countenance were as serene and undisturbed as if he were merely looking forward

186

to the peaceable humdrum of a farmer's winter. The appearance of fields and forests past which the train hurried him did not depress him as they did his son ; a shabby farm-house merely made him thank heaven that his own was more sightly and comfortable ; a bit of pine-barren or scrub-oak reminded him, to his great satisfaction, that his own woodland could be trusted to pay some profit, to say nothing of taxes and interest. Even swampy lowlands caused his heart to warm with pride that his strong arm and stronger will had transformed similar bogs into ground more fertile than some to which nature had been kinder.

Nor did he lose his serenity when the natives came down on him, like a famished horde of locusts, and demanded news of what was going on in the city. He cheerfully told them nearly everything he knew, and parried undesirable questions without losing his temper. He pointed with pride to his sub-soil plough and his wife's new bread-pan, and told how the lenses in his new spectacles had been made to equalize the strength of his eyes, instead of being both alike, as in the glasses at the village stores. He had heard all the great preachers, had a good square talk with the commission-merchant to whom most Haynton farm-products went, seen everything that the newspapers advertised as wonderfully cheap, bought some seed oats larger than any ever seen in Haynton, got a Sunday hat which was neither too large nor too small, too young nor too old, and added to the family collection of pictures a photograph of the Washington monument and an engraving of the "Death of President Garfield."

Haynton and its environs simply quivered with excitement over all the news and personal property which the farmer brought back ; but it experienced deeper thrills when the old man told his neighbors that he knew of a plan by which they might get rid of their ridge-land for an amount of money the mere interest of which would bring them more profit than the crops coaxed from that thin soil. The plan would benefit them still more should the buyer's project succeed, for a lot of cottagers would make a brisk cash market for the vegetables which Haynton ground produced so easily, and which Haynton farmers moaned over because they could not at present sell the surplus at any price, much less at the figures which their agricultural newspapers told them were to be obtained in large cities.

Would they take ten dollars per acre for their ridge-land, the money to be forfeited unless the remainder of two hundred per acre were paid within a year? Would they? Well, they consented with such alacrity that the farmer soon had to write to New York for more currency. Before Thanksgiving Day the Haynton Bay Improvement Company controlled a full mile of shore front, and there was more money in circulation in the village than could be remembered except by the oldest inhabitant, who was reminded of the good old times when in 1813 a privateer, built and manned in Haynton's little bay, had carried a rich prize into New York and come home to spend the proceeds. Small mortgages were paid off, dingy houses appeared in new suits of paint, several mothers in Israel bought new Sun-

day dresses, two or three farmers gave their old horses
and some money for better ones, the aisle of one
church was carpeted and another church obtained
the bell that for years had been longed for, a veteran pastor had fifty dollars added to his salary of
four hundred a year, and got the money, too, several
families began to buy parlor-organs, on the instal-
ment plan, one farmer indulged in the previously
unheard-of extravagance of taking his family, consisting of his wife and himself, to New York to spend
the winter, and another dedicated his newly-found
money and his winter-enforced leisure to the repre-
hensible work of drinking himself to death.

"An' it's all on account of a gal," farmer Hayn
would remark to his wife whenever he heard of any
new movement that could be traced to the ease of
the local money market. "If our Phil hadn't got
that Tramlay gal on the brain last summer, he
wouldn't have gone to New York to visit; then I
wouldn't have gone to look for him, and the Improvement Company wouldn't have been got up, an' Phil
wouldn't have hatched the brilliant idea of buyin'—
what did he call 'em?—oh, yes; options—buyin'
options on the rest of the ridge, an' there would have
been no refreshin' shower of greenbacks fallin' like
the rain from heaven on the just an' unjust alike.
It reminds me of the muss that folks got into in the
old country over that woman Helen, whose last name
I never could find out. You remember it?—'twas
in the book that young minister we had on trial,
an' didn't exactly like, left at our house. It's just
another such case, only a good deal more proper,

this not bein' a heathen land. All on account of a gal !'"

"If it is," Mrs. Hayn replied on one occasion, as she took her hands from the dough she was kneading, "an' it certainly looks as if it was, don't you think it might be only fair to allude to her more respectful ? I don't like to hear a young woman that our Phil's likely to marry spoke of as just 'that Tramlay gal.'"

"S'pose, then, I mention her as your daughter-in-law ? But ain't it odd that all the changes that's come to pass in the last month or two wouldn't have happened at all if it hadn't been for Phil's bein' smitten by that gal ? As the Scripture says, 'Behold how great a matter a little fire kindleth.' For 'fire' read 'spark,' or sparkin', an' the text——"

"Reuben !" exclaimed Mrs. Hayn, "don't take liberties with the Word."

"It ain't no liberty," said the old man. "Like enough it'll read 'spark' iu the Revised Edition."

"Then wait till it does, or until you're one of the revisers," said the wife.

"All right ; mebbe it would be as well," the husband admitted. "Meanwhile, I don't mind turnin' it off an' comparin' it with another text : 'The wind bloweth where it listeth, but thou canst not tell whence it cometh or whither it goeth.' The startin' up of Haynton an' of Phil's attachment is a good deal like——"

"I don't know that that's exactly reverent, either," said Mrs. Hayn, "considerin' what follers in the Book. An' what's goin' on in the neighborhood don't interest me as much as what's goin' on in my

own family. I'd like to kuow when things is comin'
to a head. Phil ain't married, nor even engaged,
that we know of; there ain't no lots bein' sold by the
company, or if there are we don't hear about it."

"An' there's never any bread bein' baked while
you're kneadin' the dough, old lady. You remember
the passage, 'first the blade, then the ear, then the
full corn in the ear'? Mustn't look for fruit in
blossomin'-time : even Jesus didn't find that when he
looked for it on a fig-tree ahead of time, you know."

"'Pears to me you run to Scripture more than usual
this mornin'," said Mrs. Hayn, after putting her pans
of dough into the oven. "What's started you?"

"Oh, only a little kind of awakenin', I s'pose,"
said the old man. "I can't keep my mind off of
what's goin' on right under my eyes, an' it's so unlike what anybody would have expected that I can't
help goin' behind the returns, as they used to say in
politics. An' when I do that there's only one way
of seein' 'em, an' I'm glad I've got the eyes to see
'em in that light."

"So am I," said Mrs. Hayn, gently but successfully
putting a floury impression of four fingers and a
thumb on her husband's head. "I s'pose it's 'cause
I'm so tired of waitin' that I don't look at things
just as you do. 'Pears to me there's nothin' that
comes up, an' that our hearts get set on, but what
we've got to wait for. It gets to be awful tiresome,
after you've been at it thirty or forty years. I think
Phil might hurry up matters a little."

"Mebbe 'tisn't Phil's fault," suggested the farmer.

"Well," said Mrs. Hayn, with a flash behind her

glasses, "I don't see why any gal should keep *that* boy a-waitin', if that's what you mean."

"Don't, eh?" drawled the old man, with a queer smile and a quizzical look. "Well, I s'pose he *is* a good deal more takin' than his father was."

"No such thing," said the old lady.

"Much obliged : I'm a good deal too polite to contradict,—when you're so much in earnest, you know," the old man replied. "But if it's so, what's the reason that you kept *him* waitin'?"

"Why, I—it was—you see, I—'twas—the way of it was—sho!" And Mrs. Hayn suddenly noticed that a potted geranium in the kitchen window needed a dead leaf removed from its base.

"Yes," said her husband, following her with his eyes. "An' I suppose that's just about what Phil's gal would say, if any one was to ask her. But the longer you waited the surer I was of you, wasn't I?"

"Oh, don't ask questions when you know the answer as well as I do," said the old lady. "I want to see things come to a head; that's all."

"They'll come; they'll come," said the old man. "It's tryin' to wait, I know, seein' I'm doin' some of the waitin' myself; but 'the tryin' of your faith worketh patience,' an' 'let patience have her perfect work,' you remember."

"More Scripture!" sighed the wife. "You're gettin' through a powerful sight of New Testament this mornin', Reuben, an' I s'pose I deserve it, seein' the way I feel like fightin' it. But s'pose this company speculation don't come to anythin'? then Phil'll be a good deal wuss off than he is now, won't he?

You remember the awful trouble Deacon Trewk got into by bein' the head of that new-fangled stump- and stone-puller company, that didn't pull any to speak of. Everybody came down on him, an' called him all sorts of names, an' said he'd lied to 'em, an' they would go to the poor-house because of the money they'd put in it on his advice, an'——"

"Phil won't have any such trouble," said the farmer, "for nobody took stock on his advice. Tram- lay got up the company, before we knew anythin' about it, an' all the puffin' of the land was done by him. Besides, there's nobody in it that'll suffer much, even if things come to the wust. Except one or two dummies,—clerks of Tramlay's,—who were let in for a share or two, just to make up a Board of Directors to the legal size, what shares ain't held by Phil and Tramlay an' that feller Marge belongs to a gal."

"What? Lucia?"

"No, no,—another gal : mebbe I ought to call her a woman, seein' she's putty well along, although mighty handsome an' smart. Her name's Dinon, an' Tramlay joked Phil about her once or twice, makin' out she was struck by him, but of course that's all nonsense. She's rich, an' got money to invest every once in a while, an' Tramlay put her up to this little operation."

"You're sure she ain't interested in Phil?" asked Mrs. Hayn. "I've seen no end of trouble made between young folks by gals that's old enough to know their own minds an' smart enough to use 'em."

"For goodness' sake, Lou Ann !" exclaimed the old farmer. "To hear you talk, anybody would s'pose

I   n   17

that in the big city of New York, where over a million
people live and a million more come in from diff'rent
places every week, there wasn't any young man for
folks to get interested in but our Phil. Reelly, old
lady, I'm beginnin' to be troubled about you; that
sort of feelin' that's croppin' out all the time in you
makes me afeard that you've got a kind o' pride
that's got to have a fall,—a pride in our son, settin'
him above all other mortal bein's, so far as anythin's concerned that can make a young man in-
terestin'."

"Well," said Mrs. Hayn, after apparently thinking
the matter over, "if it's so I reckon it'll have to stay
so. I don't b'lieve there's any hope of forgiveness
for anythin' if heaven's goin' to hold an old woman
to account for seein' all the good there is in her first-
born. I hain't been down to York myself, but some
of York's young sprigs have been down here, one
time an' another, an' if they're fair samples of the
hull lot, I should think a sight of our Phil would be
to all the city gals like the shadder of a great rock in
a weary land."

"Who's a-droppin' into Scripture now?" asked the
old farmer, moving to where he could look his wife
full in the face.

"Scripture ain't a bit too strong to use freely about
our Phil,—my Phil," said the old woman, pushing
her spectacles to the top of her head and beginning
to walk the kitchen floor. "All the hopin', an'
fearin', an' waitin', an' nursin', an' teachin', an'
thinkin', an' prayin', that that boy has cost comes
hurryin' into my mind when I think about him. If

there's anythin' he ought to be an' isn't, I don't see what it is, an' I can't see where his mother's to blame for it. Whatever good there is in me I've tried to put into him, an' whatever I was lackin' in I've tried to get for him elsewhere. You've been to him ev'rythin' a father should, an' he never could have got along without you. You've been lots to him that I never could be, he bein' a boy, an' I never cease thankin' heaven for it; but whenever my mind gets on a strain about him I kind o' get us mixed up, an' feel as if 'twas me instead of him that was takin' whatever happened, an' the longer it lasts the less I can think of him any other way. There!"

The old farmer rose to his feet while this speech was under way; then he removed his hat, which he seldom did after coming into the house, unless reminded. When his wife concluded, he took both her hands and dropped upon his knees; he had often done it before,—years before, when overcome by her young beauty,—but never before had he done it with so much of reverence.

CHAPTER XXII.

SEVERAL GREEN-EYED MONSTERS.

As the season hurried toward the Christmas holidays, there came to Philip Hayn the impression that he was being seen so much in public with Lucia, never against that young lady's inclination, that perhaps some people were believing him engaged to her, or sure to be. This impression became more distinct when some of his new business-acquaintances rallied or complimented him, and when he occasionally declined an invitation, given *viva voce*, by explaining that he had promised to escort Miss Tramlay somewhere that evening. If this explanation were made to a lady, as was usually the case, a knowing smile, or at least a significant look, was almost sure to follow : it began to seem to Phil that the faces of the young women of New York said a great deal more than their tongues, and said it in a way that could not be answered, which was quite annoying. If he was to seem engaged, he would prefer that appearances might not be deceitful. Again and again he was on the point of asking the question which he little doubted would be favorably answered, but he always restrained himself by the reminder that he was only a clerk on a salary that could not support a wife, bred like Lucia, in New

York, and that villa plots at Haynton Bay were not selling as rapidly as they should if he were to become well-to-do; indeed, they scarcely were selling at all. Who could be expected to become interested in building-sites on the sea-shore when even in the sheltered streets of the city the wind was piercing the thickest overcoats? And who could propose to a girl while another man, even were he that stick Marge, was offering her numerous attentions, all of which she accepted?—confound Marge and his money!

That Marge also was jealous was inevitable. Highly as he valued himself, he knew womankind well enough to imagine that a handsome young fellow just past his majority might be more gratifying to the eye, at least, than a man who had reached— well, who had not mentioned his age since he passed his thirty-fifth birthday. He had in his favor all the prestige of a good record in society, of large acquaintance and aristocratic extraction, but he could not blind himself to the fact that the young women who were most estimable did not greet him as effusively and confidentially as they did Phil. His hair was provokingly thin on the top of his head, and farther back there was a **tell-tale** spot that resembled a tonsure; he could not quickly enter, like Phil, into the spirit of some silly, innocent frolic, and although he insisted that his horses were as good as Phil's, he could not bring himself to extending an invitation for a morning dash through the Park, as Phil did once or twice a week. So he frequently said to himself, Confound the country habit of early rising, which his rival had evidently mastered.

17*

As for Lucia, except for the few happy hours she spent with Phil, and the rather more numerous hours devoted to day-dreams regarding her youthful swain, she was really miserable in her uncertain condition. Other girls were getting engaged, on shorter acquaintance, and ten times as many girls were tormenting her with questions as to which of the two was to be the happy man. She devoutly wished that Phil would speak quickly, and finally, after a long and serious consultation with Margie, she determined to adopt toward Phil the tactics which only two or three months before she had tried on Marge : she would encourage his rival. With Marge it had had the unexpected effect of making her yield her heart to Phil ; on the other hand, it had perceptibly quickened Marge's interest in her : would not a reversal of the factors have a corresponding result?

She had but one fear, but that was growing intense. Agnes Dinon continued to be fond of Phil ; there was no other man to whom she ever saw Agnes appear so cheerful and unconstrained. Could it be that the heiress was playing a deep game for the prize that to Lucia seemed the only one in view? She had seen wonderful successes made by girls as old as Agnes, when they had any money as a reserve force, and she trembled as she thought of the possibilities. Agnes was old,—dreadfully old,—it seemed to Lucia, but she was undeniably handsome, her manners were charming, and she was smart beyond compare. She had declared that her interest in Phil was only in his position as Lucia's admirer ; but—people did not always tell the truth when they were in love. Lucia

herself had told a number of lies—the very whitest
of white lies—about her own regard for Phil: suppose
Agnes were doing likewise? If she were—— Lucia's
little finger-nails made deep prints on the palms of
her hands as she thought of it.

She told herself, in her calmer moments, that such
a thought was unworthy of her and insulting to.
Agnes, who really had been friendly and even affectionate to her. In wakeful hours at night, however,
or in some idle hours during the day, she fell into
jealousy, and each successive tumble made her thral-
dom the more hopeless. She tried to escape by
rallying Phil about Agnes, but the young man, sup-
posing her to be merely playful in her teasing, did
his best to continue the joke, and was utterly blind
to the results.

At last there came an explosion. At a party which
was to Lucia unspeakably stupid, there being no
dancing, Miss Dinon monopolized Phil for a full
hour,—a thousand hours, it seemed to Lucia,—and
they sat on a sofa, too, that was far retired, in an end
of a room which once had been a conservatory.
Lucia watched for an opportunity to demand an
explanation: it seemed it never would come, but
finally an old lady who was the head and front of a
small local missionary effort in the South called the
young man aside. In an instant Lucia seated herself
beside Agnes Dinon, saying, as she gave her fan a
vicious twitch,—

"You seem to find Mr. Hayn very entertaining?"

"Indeed I do," said Miss Dinon, "I haven't spent
so pleasant an hour this season, until this evening."

"Oh!" exclaimed Lucia, and the unoffending fan flew into two pieces.

"My dear girl!" exclaimed Agnes, picking up one of the fragments. "It's really wicked to be so careless."

"Thank you," said Lucia, with a grand air—for so small a woman. "I thought it was about time for an apology."

Miss Dinon looked sidewise in amazement.

"The subject of conversation must have been delightful," Lucia continued.

"Indeed it was," said Agnes.

Lucia looked up quickly. Fortunately for Miss Dinon, the artificial light about them was dim.

"You told me once," said Lucia, collecting her strength for a grand effort, "that——"

"Yes?"

"That—that——"

"You dear little thing," said Agnes, suddenly putting her arm about Lucia and pressing her closely as a mother might seize a baby, "what we were talking of was you. Can't you understand, now, why I enjoyed it so much?"

There was a tremor and a convulsive movement within the older woman's arm, and Lucia seemed to be crying.

"Darling little girl," murmured Agnes, kissing the top of Lucia's head; "I ought to be killed for teasing you, even for a moment, but how could you be jealous of me? Your lover has been a great deal more appreciative: he has done me the honor to make me his confidante, and again I say it was delightful."

"I'm awfully mean," sobbed Lucia.

"Stop crying—at once," whispered Agnes. "How will your eyes look? Oh, Lu, what a lucky girl you are!"

"For crying?" said Lucia, after a little choke.

"For having such a man to adore you. Why, he thinks no such woman ever walked the earth before. He worships the floor you tread, the air you breathe, the rustle of your dress, the bend of your little finger, the——"

The list of adorable qualities might have been prolonged had not a little arm suddenly encircled Miss Dinon's waist so tightly that further utterance was suspended. Then Lucia murmured,—

"The silly fellow! I'm not half good enough for him."

"Do you really think so?"

"Indeed I do; I do, really."

"I'm so glad to hear you say so," said the older girl, "for, honestly, Lu, Mr. Hayn has so much head and heart that he deserves the best woman alive."

"It's such a comfort to be told so!" murmured the younger girl.

"One would suppose you had doubted it, and needed to be assured," said Agnes, with a quizzical smile.

"Oh, no! 'twasn't that," said Lucia, hurriedly. "How could you think of such a thing? But—— Oh, Agnes, you can't understand, not having been in love yourself."

Miss Dinon looked grave for an instant, but was quickly herself again, and replied, with a laugh, and a pinch bestowed upon the tip of Lucia's little car,—

"True; true. What depths of ignorance we poor old maids are obliged to grope in !"

"Now, Agnes!" pleaded Lucia. "You know I didn't mean to be offensive. All I meant was that you—that I—— Oh, I think he's all goodness and sense and brightness and everything that's nice, but—and so, I mean, I like to hear about it from everybody. I want to hear him talked of all the while; and you won't think me silly for it, will you? Because he really deserves it. I don't believe there's his equal on the face of the earth !"

"I've heard other girls talk that way about their lovers," said Agnes, "and I've been obliged to hope their eyes might never be opened; but about the young man who is so fond of you I don't differ with you in the least. He ought to marry the very best woman alive."

"Don't say that, or I shall become jealous again. He ought to find some one like you; while I'm nothing in the world but a well-meaning little goose."

"The daughter of your parents can't be anything so dreadful, even if she tries; and all young girls seem to try, you know. But you really aren't going to be satisfied to marry Philip Hayn and be nothing but a plaything and a pretty little tease to him, are you? It's so easy to stop at that; so many girls whom I know have ceased to grow or improve in any way after marriage. They've been so anxious to be cunning little things that they've never become even women. It makes one almost able to forgive the ancients for polygamy, to see——"

"Agnes Dinon ! How can you be so dreadful?"

"To see wives go on year after year, persisting in being as childish as before they were married, while their husbands are acquiring better sense and taste every year."

Lucia was sober and silent for a moment; then she said,—

"Do you know, Agnes,—I wouldn't dare to say it to any other girl,—do you know there are times when I'm positively afraid of Phil? He does know so much. I find him delightful company,—stop smiling in that astonished way, you. dear old hypocrite!—I mean I find him delightful company even when he's talking to me about things I never was much interested in. And what else is there for him to talk about? He's never proposed, you know, and, though I can't help seeing he is very fond of me, he doesn't even talk about love. But it is when he and papa get together and talk about what is going on in the world that I get frightened; for he does know so much. It isn't only I that think so, you know: papa himself says so: he says he finds it pays better to chat with Phil than to read the newspapers. Now, you know, the idea of marrying a—a sort of condensed newspaper would be just too dreadful."

"Husbands who love their wives are not likely to be condensed newspapers,—not while they are at home: but do train yourself to be able to talk to your husband of something besides the petty affairs of all of your mutual acquaintances. I have met some persons of the masculine persuasion who were so redolent of the affairs of the day as to be dreadful bores: if they wearied me in half an hour, what must their poor wives endure? But don't imagine that men are the only sinners in this respect. There isn't in existence a more detestable, unendurable, condensed newspaper—thank you for the expression—than the young wife who in calling and receiving calls absorbs all the small gossip and scandal of a large circle, and unloads it at night upon a husband who is too courteous to protest and too loyal, or perhaps merely too weary, to run away. I don't wonder that a great many married men frequently spend evenings at the clubs: even the Southern slaves used to have two half-holidays a week, besides Sunday."

"Agnes Dinon! To hear you talk, one would suppose you were going to cut off your hair and write dreadful novels under a mannish name."

- "On the contrary, I'm very proud of my long hair and of everything else womanly, especially in sweet girls who are in love. As for writing novels, I'm afraid, from the way I've been going on for the past few moments, that sermonizing, or perhaps lecturing, would be more in the line of my gifts. And the company are going down to the dining-room: there's a march playing, and I see Phil struggling toward you. You're a dear little thing to listen to me so patiently, but you'll be dearer yet if you'll remember all I've said. You're going to have a noble husband; do prepare yourself to be his companion and equal, so he may never tire of you. Hosts of husbands weary of wives who are nothing but sweet. Even girls can't exist on candy alone, you know."

CHAPTER XXIII.

E. & W.

WHEN iron looked up, as recorded elsewhere in this narrative, there was at the same time much looking up done or attempted by various railroad-companies. To some of them the improved prospects of iron were due; others were merely hopeful and venturesome; but that portion of the general public which regards a railroad only as a basis for the issue of stock in which men can speculate did not distinguish between the two.

Like iron and railroads, stocks also began to look up, and Mr. Marge devoted himself more closely than ever to the quotations which followed each other moment by moment on the tape of the stock-ticker. It seemed never safe for him to be out of hearing of the instrument, for figures changed so suddenly and unexpectedly; shares in some solid old roads about which everybody knew everything remained at their old figures, while some concerns that had only just been introduced in Wall Street, and were as problematic as new acquaintances in general, figured largely in the daily reports of Stock Exchange transactions.

Mr. Marge remembered previous occasions of similar character: during the first of them he had been a "lamb," and was sheared so closely and rudely that

he afterward took great interest in the shearing pro-
cess, perhaps to improve and reform it. He was not
at all misled by the operations on the street at the
period with which this story concerns itself; he knew
that some of the new securities were selling for more
than they were worth, that the prices of others, and
the great volume of transactions in them, were made
wholly by brokers whose business it was to keep
them before the people.   Others, which seemed
promising, could fulfil their hopes only on certain
contingencies.

   Yet Marge, cool and prudent though he was, took
no interest whatever in "securities" that deserved
their name ; he devoted all his attention to such
stocks as fluctuated wildly,—stocks about which con-
flicting rumors, both good and bad, came day by day,
sometimes hour by hour. He did not hesitate to inform himself that he was simply a gambler, at the
only gentlemanly game which the law did not make
disreputable, and that the place for his wits and
money was among the stocks which most indulged
in "quick turns" and to which the outside public—
the great flock of lambs—would be most attracted.

   After a careful survey of the market, and several
chats, apparently by chance, with alleged author-
ities of the street, he determined to confine his
operations to the stock of "The Eastern and Western
Consolidated Railway Company," better known on
the street and the stock-tickers' tapes as "E. & W."
This stock had every feature that could make any
alleged security attractive to operators, for there was
a great deal of it, the company was formed by the

consolidation, under the guise of leasing, of the property of several other companies, it was steadily picking up small feeders and incorporating them with the main line, it held some land-grants of possible value, and, lastly, some of the managers were so brilliant, daring, and unscrupulous that startling changes in the quotations might occur at any time at very short notice. Could a gambler ask for a more promising game?

E. & W. soon began to justify Marge in his choice. For the first few days after he ventured into it the stock crept up by fractions and points so that by selling out and promptly re-purchasing Marge was able to double his investment, "on a margin," from his profits alone. A temporary break frightened him a little, but on a rumor that the company was obtaining a lease of an important connecting link he borrowed enough money to buy more instead of selling, and as—for a wonder—the rumor proved true, he "realized" enough to take a couple of hundred shares more. Success began to manifest itself in his countenance and his manner, and to his great satisfaction he once heard his name coupled with that of one of the prominent operators in the stock.

His success had also the effect of making his plans more expansive and aspiring. Should E. & W. go on as it was going, he must within half a year become quite well off,—almost rich, in fact. Such being the case, might it not be a mistake for him to attach as much importance as he had done to the iron-business and its possible effect upon the dower of Miss Tramlay? She was a charming girl, but money ought to marry money, and what would be a share of the forty or fifty thousand a year that Tramlay might make in a business which, after all, could have but the small margin of profit which active competition would allow? There were rich families toward whose daughters he had not previously dared to raise his eyes, for their heads would have demanded a fuller financial exhibit than he cared to make on the basis of the few thousands of dollars which he had invested in profitable tenement-house property. As a large holder of E. & W. his position would be different; for were not the heads of these various families operating in E. & W. themselves?

Little by little he lessened his attentions to Lucia, and his visits to the house became fewer. To Phil, who did not know the cause, the result was quickly visible, and delightful as well. The only disquieting effect was that Mrs. Tramlay's manner perceptibly changed to an undesirable degree. That prudent lady continued to inform her husband that there seemed to be no movement in Haynton Bay villa plots, and that the persistency of the young man from the country seemed to have the effect of discouraging Mr. Marge, who really had some financial standing.

The change in Marge's manner was perceptible throughout the Tramlay family. Even Margie experienced a sense of relief, and she said one evening to Lucia,—

"Isn't it lovely that your old beau is so busy in Wall Street nowadays? He doesn't come here half as much as he used to, and I don't have to be bored

by him while you're talking to Phil. You ought to
fit up a room especially for me in your new house, Lu,
for I've endured a dreadful lot for your sake."

"You silly child," Lucia replied, "you might catch
Mr. Marge yourself, if you liked. Mamma seems to
want to have him in the family."

"Thank you for the 'if,'" Margie retorted, "but I
don't care for a husband almost old enough to be my
grandfather, after being accustomed to seeing a real
nice, handsome young man about the house."

"He has money," said Lucia, "and that is what
most girls are dying to marry. Papa says he is
making a fortune if he is as deep in the market as
some folks say."

"I hope he is," said Margie. "He ought to have
something besides a wooden face, and a bald head,
and the same set of speeches and manners for all
occasions. What a splendid sphinx he would make,
or an old monument! Maybe he isn't quite antique
enough, but for vivacity he isn't any more remarkable than a stone statue. Just think of what Phil has
saved us from !"

And still E. & W. went up. The discovery of valuable mineral deposits on the line of one of its branches
sent the stock flying up several points in a single day,
and soon afterward a diversion of some large grain-
shipments from a parallel line helped it still further.
That the grain was carried at a loss did not trouble
any one,—probably because only the directors knew
it, and it was not their business to make such facts
public. And with each rise of the stock Marge sold out,
so as to have a larger margin with which to operate.

At the first of the year E. & W. declared a dividend so large, for a security that had been far below par, that even prudent investors began to crowd to the street and buy the stock to put into their safes. The effect of this was to send shares up so rapidly and steadily that Marge had difficulty in repurchasing at the price at which he sold ; but he did so well that more than six thousand shares now stood in his name on the books of his broker. Six thousand shares represented about half a million dollars, at the price which E. & W. commanded. Marge admitted to himself that it did not mean so much to him, for he had not a single certificate in his pocket or anywhere else. But what were stock certificates to a man who operated on a margin? They were good enough for widows and orphans and other people incapable or unwilling to watch the market and who were satisfied to draw annually whatever dividends might chance to be declared. To Marge the stock as it appeared on his broker's books signified that he had cleared nearly fifty thousand dollars on it within two months ; and all this money was reinvested—on margin—in the same stock, with the probability of doubling itself every month until E. & W. should go quite a way beyond par. Were it to creep up only five per cent. a month—it had been doing more than twice as well—he could figure up a cool million of gain before the summer dulness should strike the market. Then he would sell out, run over to Europe, and take a rest : he felt that he would have earned it by that time.

Of course there was no danger that E. & W. would go down. Smart, who, in the parlance of the street, was "taking care of it," had publicly said, again and again, that E. & W. would reach one hundred and fifty before summer; and, although Smart was one of the younger men in the street, he had engineered two or three other things in a manner which had made older operators open their eyes and check-books. Smart's very name seemed to breed luck, his prophecies about other movements had been fulfilled, he evidently had his own fortune largely invested in E. & W., so what more could any operator ask? Even now the stock was hard to get; investors who wanted small quantities had generally to bid above the market-quotations; and even when a large block changed hands it depressed quotations only a fraction, which would be more than recovered within twenty-four hours. Marge's margin was large enough to protect him against loss, even should a temporary panic strike the market and depress everything by sympathy: indeed, some conservative brokers told Marge that he could safely carry the stock on a much smaller margin.

Better men have had their heads turned by less success, and forgotten not only tender sentiments but tender vows: so it is no wonder that, as his financial standing improved daily, Marge's interest in Lucia weakened. The countryman might have her; there was as good fish in the sea as that he had hoped to catch,—not only as good, but a great deal better. He would not break old friendships, he really esteemed the Tramlays, but—friendship was a near enough relationship.   -

CHAPTER XXIV.

IRON LOOKS STILL HIGHER.

"Well, my dear," said Tramlay to his wife one evening in late winter, "the spell is broken. Three different people have bought building-sites of the Haynton Bay Company, and a number of others seem interested. There's been a good deal of money made this winter, and now people seem anxious to spend it. It's about time for us to be considering plans for our villa,—eh?"

"Not until we are sure we shall have more than three neighbors," said Mrs. Tramlay. "Besides, I would first like to have some certainty as to how large our family will be this summer."

"How large? Why, the same size as usual, I suppose. Why shouldn't it be?"

"Edgar," said Mrs. Tramlay, impatiently, "for a man who has a business reputation for quick wits, I think you're in some things the stupidest person who ever drew breath."

Tramlay seemed puzzled. His wife finally came to his aid, and continued:

"I should like to know if Lucia's affair is to dawdle along as it has been doing. June is as late in the season as is fashionable for weddings, and an engagement——"

212

"Oh !" interrupted the merchant, with a gesture of annoyance, "I've heard the customary talk about mother-love, and believed it, up to date, but I can't possibly bring myself to be as anxious as you to get rid of our blessed first-born."

"It is because I love her that I am so desirous of seeing her happy and settled,—not to get rid of her."

"Yes, I suppose so; and I'm a brute," said the husband. "Well, if Phil has been waiting until he should be certain about his own condition financially, he will not need to wait much longer. I don't know whether it's through brains, or tact, or what's called lover's luck, but he's been doing so well among railroad-people that in common decency I must either raise his salary largely or give him an interest in the business."

"Well, really, you speak as if the business depended upon him."

"For a month or two he's been taking all the orders; I've been simply a sort of clerk, to distribute them among mills, or find out where iron could be had for those who wanted it in haste. He's after an order now—from the Lake and Gulfside Road—that I let him attempt at first merely to keep him from growing conceited. It seemed too great and difficult a job to place any hope on; but I am beginning to half believe he'll succeed. If he does, I'll simply be compelled to give him an interest in the business: if I don't, some of my competitors will coax him away from me."

"What! after all you have done for him?"

"Tut! tut! the favor is entirely on the other side. Had some outsider brought me the orders which that boy has taken, I would have had to pay twenty times as much in commissions as Phil's salary has amounted to. What do you think of ' Edgar Tramlay & Co.' for a business sign, or even 'Tramlay & Hayn'?"

"I suppose it will have to be," said the lady, without any indication of gratification, "and, if it must be, the sooner the better, for it can't help making Lucia's position more certain. If it doesn't do so at once, I shall believe it my duty to speak to the young man."

"Don't! don't, I implore!" exclaimed the merchant. "He will think——"

"What he may think is of no consequence," said Mrs. Tramlay. "It is time that he should know what city etiquette demands."

"But it isn't necessary, is it, that he should know how matter-of-fact and cold-hearted we city people can be about matters which country-people think should be approached with the utmost heart and delicacy? Don't let him know what a mercenary, self-serving lot of wretches we are, until he is so fixed that he can't run away."

"Edgar, the subject is not one to be joked about, I assure you."

"And I assure you, my dear, that I'm not more than half joking,—not a bit more."

"I shall not say more than thousands of the most loving and discreet mothers have been obliged to say in similar circumstances," said Mrs. Tramlay. "If

you cannot trust me to discharge this duty delicately,
perhaps you will have the kindness to undertake it
yourself."

"The very thing!" said Tramlay. "If he must
have unpleasant recollections of one of us, I would
rather it wouldn't be his mother-in-law. The weight
of precedent is against you, don't you know?—though
not through any fault of yours."

"Will you seriously promise to speak to him? At
once?—this very week?"

"I promise," said Tramlay, solemnly, at the same
time wickedly making a number of mental reserva-
tions.

"Then if there should be any mistake it will not
be too late to recall poor Mr. Marge," said Mrs. Tramlay.

"My dear wife," said Tramlay, tenderly, "I know
Marge has some good qualities, but I beg you to remember that by the time our daughter ought to be
in the very prime of her beauty and spirits, unless
her health fails, Marge will be nearly seventy years
old. I can't bear the thought of our darling being
doomed to be nurse to an old man just when she will
be most fit for the companionship and sympathy of
a husband. Suppose that ten years ago, when you
boasted you didn't feel a day older than when you
were twenty, I had been twenty years older than I
am now, and hanging like a dead weight about your
neck? Between us we have had enough to do in
bringing up our children properly : what would you
have done had all the responsibility come upon you
alone? And you certainly don't care to think of the

probability of Lu being left a widow before she fairly reaches middle age?"

"Handsome widows frequently marry again, especially if their first husbands were well off."

"Wife!"

Mrs. Tramlay looked guilty, and avoided her husband's eye. She could not avoid his encircling arm, though, nor the meaning of his voice as he said,—

"Is there no God but society?"

"I didn't mean to," whispered Mrs. Tramlay. "All mothers are looking out for their daughters; I don't think fathers understand how necessary it is. If you had shown more interest in Lucia's future I might not have been so anxious. Fathers never seem to think that their daughters ought to have husbands."

"Fathers don't like girls to marry before they are women," said Tramlay. "Even now I wish Lu might not marry until she is several years older."

"Mercy!" exclaimed Mrs. Tramlay. "Would you want the poor child to go through several more years of late parties, and dancing, and dressing? Why, she'd become desperate, and want to go into a nunnery or become a novelist, or reformer, or something."

"What? Is society really so dreadful to a young girl?" asked the husband.

"It's the most tiresome thing in the world after the novelty wears off," said Mrs. Tramlay, "unless she is fond of flirting, or gets into one of the prosy sets where they talk about nothing but books and music and pictures and blue china and such things."

"'Live and learn,'" quoted the merchant. "Next time I become a young man and marry I'll bring up my family in the country. My sisters had at least horses and trees and birds and flowers and chickens to amuse them, and not one of them married until she was twenty-five."

Mrs. Tramlay maintained a discreet silence, for, except their admiration for their brother, Mrs. Tramlay had never been able to find a point of contact in her sisters-in-law. Tramlay slowly left the room and went to his club, informing himself, as he walked, that there were times in which a man really needed the society of men.

Meanwhile, Phil had for the twentieth time been closeted with the purchasing officials of the Lake and Gulfside Railroad,—as disagreeable and suspicious a couple as he had ever found among Haynton's assortment of expert grumblers. Had he been more experienced in business he would have been less hopeful, for, as everybody who was anybody in the iron trade knew the Lake and Gulfside had planned a branch nearly two hundred miles long, and there would be forty or fifty thousand tons of rails needed, everybody who was anybody in the iron trade was trying to secure at least a portion of the order. Phil's suggestion that Tramlay should try to secure the contract had affected the merchant about as a proposition of a child to build a house might have done ; but, to avoid depressing the young man's spirits, he had consented, and had himself gone so far as to get terms, for portions of the possible order, from men who were looking for encouragement to open their long-closed mills. Unknown to the merchant, and fortunately for Phil, one of the Lake and Gulfside purchasing agents had years before chanced to be a director in a company that placed a small order with Tramlay, and, remembering and liking the way in which it had been filled, was predisposed toward the house's new representative from the first. But Tramlay, not knowing this, laid everything to Phil's luck when the young man invaded the whist-room of the club, called Tramlay away from a table just as cards had been dealt, and exclaimed, in a hoarse whisper,—

"I've got it!"

"Got what?" asked the merchant, not over-pleased at the interruption. Phil stared so wildly that his employer continued, "Not the smallpox, I trust. What is it? Can't you speak?"

"I should think you'd know," said the young man, looking somewhat aggrieved.

"Not Lake and Gulfside?"

"Exactly that," said Phil, removing his hat and holding it just as he remembered to have seen a conqueror's hat held in a colored print of "General Scott entering the City of Mexico."

"Hurrah!" shouted the merchant, dashing to the floor the cards he held. This movement eliciting an angry protest from the table, Tramlay picked up the cards, thrust them into the hand of a lounger, said, "Play my hand for me.—Gentlemen, I must beg you to excuse me: sudden and important business," seized his hat, and hurried Phil to the street, exclaiming,—

"Sure there is no mistake about it? It seems too good to be true."

"There's no mistake about this," Phil replied,

taking a letter from his pocket. The merchant hurried to the nearest street-lamp, looked at the written order, and said,—

"My boy, your fortune is made. Do you realize what a great stroke of business this is?"

"I hope so," said Phil.

"What do you want me to do for you? Name your terms or figures."

Phil was silent, for the very good reason that he did not know how to say what was in his heart.

"Suppose I alter my sign to Tramlay & Hayn, and make you my equal partner?"

Still Phil was silent.

"Well," said the merchant, "it seemed to me that was a fair offer; but if it doesn't meet your views, speak out and say what you prefer."

"Mr. Tramlay," said the young man, trying to speak calmly, but failing most lamentably, "they say a countryman never is satisfied in a trade unless he gets something to boot."

"Very well. What shall it be?"

"Millions,—everything; that is, I wish you'd give me your daughter too."

The merchant laughed softly and shook his head. Phil started, and his heart fell.

"I don't see how I can do that," said Tramlay; "for, unless my eyes deceive me, you already have her."

"Thank heaven!" exclaimed Phil, devoutly.

"So say I," the merchant responded.

CHAPTER XXV.

E. &. W. AGAIN.

ONE of the penalties of success (according to the successful) being the malignant envy of those who have not succeeded, it is not surprising that in time there began to creep into Wall Street some stories that E. & W. was no better than it should be, nor even quite so good, and that there was no reason why the stock should be so high when solider securities were selling below par.

The management, assisted by the entire E. & W. cliquo, laughed all such " bear" stories to scorn, and when scorn seemed somewhat insufficient they greatly increased the volume of sales and maintained the price by the familiar, simple, but generally successful expedient of buying from one another through many different brokers in the stock-market. The bear party rallied within a day or two, and returned to the charge with an entirely new set of lies, besides an accidental truth or two; but the E. & W. clique was something of a liar itself, and arranged for simultaneous delivery, at different points on the street, of a lot of stories so full of new mineral developments on the line of the road, and so many new evidences of the management's shrewdness, that criticism was silenced for a while.

But bears must live as well as bulls, and the longer they remain hungry the harder they are sure to fight for their prey : so the street was soon favored with a fresh assortment of rumors. This time they concerned themselves principally with the alleged bad condition of the track and rolling stock in the West, and with doubts as to the mineral deposits said to have been discovered. The market was reminded that other railroad companies, by scores, had made all sorts of brilliant discoveries and announcements that had failed to materialize, and that some of these roads had been managed by hands that now seemed to be controlling E. & W.

Then the E. & W. management lost its ordinary temper and accused the bears of malignant falsehood. There was nothing unusual in this, in a locality where no one is ever suspected of telling the truth while he can make anything by lying. When, however, E. & W. issued invitations to large operators, particularly in the company's stock, for a special excursion over the road, with opportunities for thorough investigation, the bears growled sullenly and began to look for a living elsewhere.

The excursion-start was a grand success in the eyes of Mr. Marge, who made with it his first trip in the capacity of an investigating investor. There were men on the train to whom Marge had in other days scarcely dared to lift his eyes in Wall Street, yet now they treated him as an equal, not only socially but financially. He saw his own name in newspapers of cities through which the party passed ; his name had appeared in print before, but only among lists of guests at parties, or as usher or a bridegroom's best man at a wedding,—not as a financier. It was gratifying, too, to have presented to him some presidents of Western banks who joined the party, and be named to these financiers as one of the most prominent investors in E. & W.

He saw more, too, of his own country than ever before; his eyes and wits were quick enough to make him enter heartily into the spirit of a new enterprise or two which some of the E. & W. directors with the party were projecting. It might retard a little his accumulation of E. & W. stock, but the difference would be in his favor in the end. To "get in on the ground-floor" of some great enterprise had been his darling idea for years; he had hoped for it as unwearyingly as for a rich wife; now at last his desire was to be granted : the rich wife would be easy enough to find after he himself became rich. Unaccustomed though he was to slumbering with a jolting bed under him, his dreams in the sleeping-car were rosier than any he had known since the hair began to grow thin on the top of his head.

But as the party began to look through the car windows for the bears of the Rocky Mountains, the bears of Wall Street began to indulge in pernicious activity. They all attacked E. & W. with entirely new lots of stories, which were not denied rapidly enough for the good of the stock, for some of the more active managers of the E. & W. clique were more than a thousand miles away. Dispatches began to hurry Westward for new and bracing information, but the whole excursion-party had taken stages, a few hours before, for a three days' trip to see some of the rich mining-camps to which E. & W. had promised to build a branch. No answers being received, E. & W. began to droop ; as soon as it showed decided signs of weakness, and seemed to have no friends strong enough to support it, the bears sprang upon it *en masse* and proceeded to pound and scratch the life out of it. It was granted a temporary breathing-spell through the assistance of some operators in other stocks, who feared their own properties might be depressed by sympathy, but as soon as it became evident that E. & W. was to be the only sufferer all the bulls in the market sheathed their horns in bears' claws and assisted in the annihilation of the prostrate giant who had no friends.

The excursion-party returned from the mines in high spirits : even the president of the company declared he had no idea that the property was so rich. He predicted, and called all present to remember his words, that the information he would send East would "boom" E. & W. at least ten points within ten days. Marge's heart simply danced within him : if it was to be as the president predicted, his own hoped-for million by the beginning of the stagnant season would be nearer two. He smiled pityingly as Lucia's face rose before him : how strange that he had ever thought seriously of making that chit his wife, and being gratified for such dowry as the iron trade might allow her father to give !

The stages stopped at a mining-village, twenty miles from the station, for dinner. The president said to the keeper of the little hotel,—

"Is there any telegraph-station here?"

"There's a telephone 'cross the road at the store," said the proprietor. "It runs into the bankin'-house at Big Stony."

"Big Stony?" echoed the president. "Why, we've done some business with that bank. Come, gentlemen, let's go across and find out how our baby is being taken care of."

Several of the party went, Marge being among them. The president "rang up" the little bank, and bawled,—

"Got any New York quotations to-day?"

"Yes," replied a thin, far-away voice.

"How's the stock market?"

"Pretty comfortable, considering."

"Any figures on E. & W.?"

"El," was the only sound the president could evolve from the noise that followed.

"Umph!" said he; "what does that mean? 'El' must be 'twelve,'—hundred and twelve. Still rising, you see; though why it should have gone so high and so suddenly I don't exactly see. Hello," he resumed, as he turned again to the mouth-piece; "will you give me those figures again, and not quite so loud? I can't make them out."

Again the message came, but it did not seem any more satisfactory, for the president looked astonished, and then frowned; then he shouted back,—

"There's some mistake; you didn't get the right letters: I said E. & W.,—Eastern and Western. One moment. Mr. Marge, won't you kindly take my place? My hearing isn't very keen."

Marge placed the receiver to his ear, and shouted, "All right; go ahead." In two or three seconds he dropped the receiver, turned pale, and looked as if about to fall.

"What is it?" asked several voices in chorus.

"He said, 'E. & W. is dead as a smelt; knocked to pieces two days ago.'"

"What is it quoted at now?" asked one, quickly.

True enough : who could want to know more than Marge? It was in a feeble voice, though, and after two or three attempts to clear his throat, that he asked,—

"How did it close to-day?"

Again, as the answer came back, Marge dropped the receiver and acted as if about to fall.

"What is it? Speak, can't you?"

"Thirty-seven !" whispered Marge.

There was an outburst of angry exclamations, not unmixed with profanity. Then nearly all present looked at the president inquiringly, but without receiving any attempt at an explanation, for the president was far the heaviest owner of E. & W. stock, and he looked as stony of face as if he had suddenly died but neglected to close his eyes.

Marge hastily sought the outer air; it seemed to him he would lose his reason if he did not get away from that awful telephone. Thirty-seven ! he knew what that meant; his margin might have saved his own stock had the drop been to a little below par, but it had tumbled more than half a hundred points, so of course his brokers had closed the account when the margin was exhausted, and Marge, who a fort-

p

night before had counted himself worth nearly a million dollars (Wall Street millions), was now simply without a penny to his credit in Wall Street or anywhere else; what money he chanced to have in his pocket was all he could hope to call his own until the first of the next month, when the occupants of his tenement-houses would pay their rent.

It was awful; it was unendurable; he longed to scream, to rave, to tear his hair. He mentally cursed the bears, the brokers, the directors, and every one else but himself. He heard some of his companions in the store bawling messages through the telephone, to be wired to New York; these were veterans, who assumed from past experience that a partial recovery would follow and that they would partly recoup their losses. But what could he do? There was not on earth a person whom he could ask, by telegraph, for the few hundred dollars necessary to a small speculation on the ruins.

He heard the outburst of incredulity, followed by rage, as the passengers who had remained at the little hotel received the unexpected news, which now seemed to him to be days old. Then he began to suspect everybody, even the crushed president and directors. What could be easier, Marge said to himself, than for these shrewd fellows to unload quietly before they left New York, and then get out of reach so that they could not render any support in case of a break? He had heard of such things before. It certainly was suspicious that the crash should have come the very day after they got away from the telegraph-wires. Likely enough they now, through their brokers, were quietly buying up all the stock that was being offered, to "peg it up," little by little, to where it had been. The mere suspicion made him want to tear them limb from limb,—to organize a lynching-party, after the fashion of the Territory they were in, and get revenge, if not justice.

It was rather a dismal party that returned to New York from the trip over the E. & W. The president, fearing indignant Western investors, and still more the newspaper reporters, whom he knew would lie in wait for him until they found him, quietly abandoned the train before reaching Chicago, and went Eastward by some other route. A few of the more hardened operators began to encourage each other by telling of other breaks that had been the making of the men they first ruined, but they dropped their consoling reminiscences when Marge approached them; they had only contempt for a man who from his manner evidently was so completely "cleaned out" as to be unable to start again, even in a small way. The majority, however, seemed as badly off as himself; some of them were so depressed that when the stock of cigars provided specially for the excursion was exhausted they actually bought common pipes and tobacco at a way station, and industriously poisoned the innocent air for hundreds of miles.

This, then, was the end of Marge's dream of wealth! Occasionally, in other days, he had lost small sums in Wall Street, but only he and his broker knew of it; no one ever knew in what line of stock he operated. But now—why, had not his

name been printed again and again among those
of E. & W.'s strongest backers? Every one would
know of his misfortune: he could no longer pose as
a shrewd young financier, much less as a man with
as large an income as he had time to enjoy.

Would that he had not been so conceited and careless as to mentally give up Lucia, who now, for some
reason, persisted in appearing in his mind's eye!
Had he given half as much attention to her as to
E. & W., she might now be his, and their wedding-
cards might be out. And iron was still looking up,
too! How could any one not a lunatic have become
so devoted to chance as to throw away a certainty?
for she had been a certainty for him, he believed,
had he chosen to realize. Alas! with her, as with
E. & W., he had been too slow at realizing.

CHAPTER XXVI.

SOME MINDS RELIEVED.

WHEN Tramlay bade good-by to his new partner a few moments after the partnership was verbally formed he wondered which to do first,—return to the club and announce his good fortune to the several other iron men who were members, or go home and relieve the mind of his wife. As he wondered, he carelessly remarked,—

"Which way are you going, Phil?"

The young man, who was already starting off at a rapid pace, returned, and said, in a low tone,—

"Can't you imagine?"

The older man took his partner's hand, and seemed to want to say something.

"What is it, Mr. Tramlay?" asked Phil, for the silence was somewhat embarrassing.

"My dear fellow," said the merchant, "a man who has just given away his daughter is usually supposed to have done a great favor."

"As you certainly have done," Phil replied.

"Thank you; for I want to ask one in return. Fathers aren't sole proprietors of their daughters, you know. Mrs. Tramlay—when you speak to her about the affair, as of course you will, be as—be all—do be your most considerate, courteous self, won't you?"

"I beg you will trust me for that," said Phil.

"I'm sure I can,—or could, if you understood mothers as well as some day you may."

"I have a mother, you know," suggested Phil.

"True, but she had no daughters, I believe? Mothers and daughters—well, they're not exactly like mothers and sons. Mrs. Tramlay respects you highly, I know, but she may not have seemed as friendly to your suit as you could have liked. Try to forget that, won't you?—and forgive it, if it has made you uncomfortable?"

"I would forgive a bitter enemy to-night, if I had one," said the excited youth.

"That's right; that's right: a man has so few chances to feel that way that he ought to improve them all. You'll even be patient, should it be necessary?"

"As patient as Job," promised Phil.

"Thank you! God bless you!" said the merchant, wringing Phil's hand and turning away. Phil again started. The merchant walked toward the club, stopped after taking a few steps, looked in the direction Phil had taken, drew his hat down over his eyes, hurried to his house, entered the basement door, sneaked up the back stairway as if he were a thief, and quietly entered his own room, which, to his great relief, was empty.

Meanwhile, Phil had reached the house and been admitted. He had not to ask for Lucia, for he heard through the open door of the parlor some piano-chords which he knew were touched only by her fingers. Lucia did not hear him enter, and as he stopped to look at her she seemed to be in a revery that was not cheerful. He had never seen her looking so—so plain, he would have said, had she been any one else. There was no color in her face, and her cheeks seemed thin and drawn. An involuntary motion startled her, and she turned, exclaiming,—

"How you frightened me!"

"I wish you might punish me in some way for it," said Phil, approaching her.

"It was so late that I did not imagine any one would call," the girl explained.

"I was quite busy in the earlier part of the evening," said Phil, "and I needed to see your father."

"Business is horrid," said Lucia. "I should think men would attend to it by daylight. Well, I believe papa went to the club."

"Yes; I found him."

"And, as usual, he sent you home for some horrid papers of some kind?"

"No, not exactly," said Phil. How uncomfortable it is to have a dream dispelled—even a day-dream! All along the way to the house he had imagined just how she would look; he could see the flush of her cheek through the half-mile of darkness that he had traversed, his path had seemed illumined by the light of her eyes, yet now she was pallid, and her eyes had none of their customary lustre, and her mental condition—it did not seem at all appropriate to the conversation which he had a hundred times imagined and upon which he had set his heart that night. Well, he would be patient: "Faint heart never won fair lady."

"Aren't you a little severe on your father for his devotion to business?" he ventured to ask. "Out in the country we have an old saying, 'Make hay while the sun shines.' The sun never shone brighter than now in the iron-business."

"Yes, I know," replied Lucia, wearily. "It's always something for business' sake. Yes, we have that same dreadful saying in New York."

"But it's all for the sake of women that men are so absorbed in business," argued Phil. "What would your father care for business, if it weren't for his wife and charming daughters and younger children? He never sees iron, I imagine, while he is talking about it, nor even thinks of the money, for its own sake. Greenbacks and gold and notes and bonds all transform themselves, in his eyes, I suppose, into dresses and cloaks and bonnets and opera-boxes and trips to Europe, and——"

"You silly fellow!" said Lucia, with the first smile upon which she had ventured that evening; "I wonder where you get such notions. If you don't give them up you will some day find yourself writing poetry,—something about the transmutation of rail-road-iron into gold. Think how ridiculous that would seem!"

"But when iron attempts 'to gild refined gold,—to paint the lily,'" said Phil, "as it does in your father's case, why, 'twould be worth dropping into poetry to tell of at least one instance where Shakespeare's conclusion was wrong. You know the rest of the quotation?"

Yes, evidently Lucia knew it, for her cheek glowed

prettily under the compliment, which, while somewhat awkward, reached its mark by the help of
Phil's eyes. As for Phil, his heart began to be itself
again: whose heart wouldn't, he asked himself,
under the consciousness of having given one second
of pleasure to that dear girl?

"You seem to be in a sermonizing mood to-night,"
said Lucia. "I know my father is the best man alive,
and I supposed you liked him,—a little; but I can't
imagine what should have impressed you so strongly
with him to-night."

Phil studied the toes of his boots, the tints of the
patternless rug, the design of the frescoed ceiling.
Lucia watched him with an amused face, and finally
said, "Even you don't seem to know."

"I know," said Phil, slowly, "and I'm trying to
think how to express it properly."

Poor fellow! how he did despise himself, that what
he had hurried there to say would not come to his
lips properly! Such a story had seemed easy enough
when he had read, in books, of how other men told
it,—so easy, indeed, that he had come to have very
little patience with that portion of novels. Of course
he could not tell it while Lucia was laughing,—
laughing at him, too. Perhaps he could lead conversation back to the desired tone; but no; for just at
that instant Margie flew into the room, exclaiming,
before she fairly entered,—

"Oh, Lu, isn't it awful? I just went across the
room for something, and my dress caught the table-
cover, and over went an inkstand on my very, veriest
white—— Why, Phil, I didn't know you were here."

20*

"I wish I knew what would take ink-stains from very, veriest white——"

"Oh, so do I. What shall I do, Lu? Do tell me at once."

"Perhaps," suggested Phil, with a gleam of hope for Margie and several for himself, "your laundress can tell."

"The very thing," said Margie. "What a blessing you are! I wish you were always here." Then she flew out of the room, but not until she had flung a meaning look at her sister and another at Phil. Both blushed, and Phil felt uncomfortable, but as he stole a look at Lucia he mentally blessed Margie, for Lucia was no longer laughing, and she was looking unusually pretty; her eyes, slightly downcast, seemed a more heavenly blue than ever.

"The reason I have your father's goodness on my mind to-night," said Phil, breaking the silence to abate the awkwardness of the situation, "is because to-night he has made me his partner in business,—his own equal."

"Oh, Phil!" exclaimed Lucia, her whole face suddenly aglow and her eyes looking full into his. "I'm so glad—so glad for you—for him, I mean; for both of you. What I meant to say was—— Oh, how did it happen?"

"Oh, I chanced to get an order which he was kind enough to think the greatest stroke of business that any firm has made this season. So he asked me my price, and while I was wondering what to say he made me the offer."

"Just like his dear, noble heart," said Lucia.

"Yes," said Phil, rising, and pacing to and fro in front of the piano, and fixing his eyes on the floor; "and all the nobler it seemed on account of the sordid, grasping way in which I took it. I wasn't satisfied with that, but wanted more. I hope he'll never have cause to think unkindly of me for it."

"More?" said Lucia, wonderingly, and somewhat soberly. "What more could you want than to be a prominent merchant?"

"As we say in the country, guess," said Phil, approaching the piano-stool and opening his arms.

Lucia guessed.

What a deal he had to say to her, while still they stood there! He knew it was not polite to keep a lady standing, but while he was supporting her so strongly, though tenderly, it did not seem that Lucia would weary of the position; nor did she. And what a lot of questions each asked and answered!—questions and answers that would seem as silly to any one else as they were interesting to those they concerned. Perhaps there came occasional moments when neither was speaking, but during these Phil could look down at the golden tangle just about at the level of his lips, and think how much more precious it was than all the gold that railroad-iron could be changed into by the alchemy of endeavor.

·How long they might have stood there, if undisturbed, they never knew, for they were so heedless of all that might be going on about them that they did not note the entrance of Margie, who was returning from an interview with the laundress in the basement. That young lady was quick to discern the situation, and was about to depart quietly and with celerity ; but, acting upon the promptings of her second thoughts, she returned, threw her arms around the couple, and exclaimed,—

"Oh, isn't this splendid !"

There was a rapid separation of the trio, and then Margie attempted to whirl Lucia about the room in a waltz, that being the younger sister's most natural method of expressing joy. But, somehow, Lucia did not feel like waltzing ; on the contrary, she kissed her sister several times, hid her own face a great deal, and finally made a great effort to be calm as she pointed at Phil and said, with a sprightly toss of her head,—

"Papa's partner. Tramlay and Hayn is to be the sign over the store hereafter."

Margie's eyes opened in amazement for a moment ; then it was Phil's turn to be whirled about the room,— an operation in which he displayed the astounding awkwardness peculiar to young men who cannot dance. Suddenly she paused, and said,—

"Mamma must know at once. The idea of there being some one within reach to tell it to, and I wasting all this time !"

"Margie !" exclaimed Lucia, as the girl's dress rustled up the stair, "Margie, come back a moment,— do." Then there was some rapid whispering, and Margie re-ascended, saying, in very resigned tones,—

"Very well."

"I suspect," said Phil, when Lucia returned, "that you've suggested that I am the proper person to break the news."

"'Isn't it better?" asked Lucia, timidly.

".Infinitely."

"Mamma is not always easy to speak to, on some subjects," Lucia suggested.

"No task could be hard to me to-night," responded Phil.

Yet in a moment or two, when Mrs. Tramlay was heard approaching, the young man's looks belied his brave words. Lucia pitied him; she pressed closely to his side, as if to assist him, but when her mother's footstep was heard in the hall the girl's courage deserted her, and she fled, and left the young man to whatever fate might be impending.

"Margie tells me you have some great news," said Mrs. Tramlay to Phil.

"Bless Margie!" said Phil to himself; then, instead of at once addressing himself to the duty before him, he gave Mrs. Tramlay as full a report of the rise, progress, and result of the Lake and Gulfside operation as if she, instead of her husband, were the head of the iron-house.

"And you have told Mr. Tramlay, I think you said," the lady remarked.

"Yes; I looked him out at the club, for the purpose."

"He was pleased, of course?"

"Greatly, I am happy to say."

Mrs. Tramlay looked thoughtful. Phil was puzzled by her manner. Did she know or care so little about business as not to estimate at its true value the importance of the Lake and Gulfside order? She was so calm about it that Phil himself began to think less than before of his success. He even wondered whether it would be worth while to tell her of the worldly fortune the operation had brought to him. Probably she was one of the large class of women, of whom he had heard, who have no heads for business.

"Did Mr. Tramlay say anything in reply?" asked the lady, after a moment or two of thought.

"Why, yes," said Phil, with some hesitation, for he wondered if, after all, it might not be better that Tramlay himself should tell the story of his clerk's promotion. Mrs. Tramlay eyed him keenly; then she asked,—

"Did he say anything concerning your future,—and ours also, as related to it?"

"Yes," said Phil, now satisfied that Tramlay's offer had been premeditated, and not made in the excitement of the moment; "and," he continued, with his best smile and bow, "I am happy to assure you that I was simply delighted to agree with him."

"My dear son!" exclaimed Mrs. Tramlay.

Phil's astonishment reached almost the stage of petrifaction, but before he could betray it his prospective mother-in-law had depressed his head so that she might kiss him on both cheeks.

Such a prayer of thanksgiving as Phil's heart sent up as he returned Mrs. Tramlay's salutation! Meanwhile, two young women who had been flagrantly transgressing one of the most imperative rules of their breeding flew at each other from the two doors that opened from the hall into the parlor: at last Margie had found some one who was both able and willing to be waltzed madly about. They were even reckless enough to float into the parlor, right before their mother's eyes. Then Mrs. Tramlay, conscious for the first time that her eyes were wet, flew to the seclusion of her own room, where, to her great surprise, she fell into the arms of her husband.

CHAPTER XXVII.

AMONG THE RUINS.

MR. MARGE reached New York with only the distinct impression that he would like at once to turn his single bit of real estate into cash, shake the dust of the city from his feet forever, and begin life and business anew at some place where he was not known, and where the disgrace—as it seemed to him—of his altered fortunes would be unknown to any one. There was his interest in the Haynton Bay property, to be sure, but he cursed the day he had ever put nearly two thousand dollars into property which at best would not be likely to return any amount of cash for years to come. He might sell that also; but who would buy it? Nobody knew much about it but the other owners; of these, two were Tramlay and Phil, to neither of whom would he admit that he needed money: he would rather lose all he had invested. As for Agnes Dinou, who held most of the remaining shares, he could not make a business-offer to a woman who had refused his hand and heart several years before.

Perhaps his broker had saved something for him from the wreck. Marge sought an obscure hotel instead of going to his apartments or his club, and, fearing even to meet any one he knew on Wall Street,
240

went to his broker's house by night. The interview was not satisfactory : the broker had not only been obliged to close Marge's account, but, infected by his customer's success, had operated so largely in E. & W. on his own account that he also had been ruined, and contemplated selling his seat in the Exchange so as to make good some of his indebtedness to members.

As for E. & W., instead of recovering it had gone lower and lower, until operations in it almost ceased. The president, utterly ruined, retired from office, turned over all his property to his creditors, and went abroad to recover his shattered health or to die, he did not much care which.

Marge sold his house at auction, and, while wearily awaiting the circumlocution of "searching title" which necessarily preceded his getting full payment, he betook himself to Boston. To avoid speculation was impossible, it had been his life for years ; and, as he found mining-shares were within his reach, he began again to operate, in a small way. The little he had seen of mines while on the fateful E. & W. excursion was so much more than the majority of those about him knew on the subject that he made a few lucky turns, and he finally interested some acquaintances in a promising silver property he had seen in the West. His acquaintances succeeded in getting the property "listed" at one of the New York exchanges, and Marge, with new hopes and a great deal of desperation, risked nearly all he had on the Brighthope mine.

The scheme worked finely for some weeks. It was

L   q   21

skilfully managed by the Bostonians interested ; they even succeeded in getting a great deal about it into the newspapers of both cities. But—alas for the wickedness of human nature !—one day the company were horrified to learn that their title to the property was hopelessly defective. When this fact became indisputable, Brighthope stock tumbled farther than E. & W.,—tumbled utterly out of sight ; and all the assets of the company, except the safe and two desks, were sold to a paper-stock dealer at a cent a pound.

Then Marge thought seriously of suicide. He had but a thousand or two dollars left: how could he operate in anything on that small sum and support himself besides? He could add something to the sum by selling his horses and carriage, but such things always had to go at a sacrifice ; besides, there would be a terrible bill to be paid for the maintenance of the animals during the two or three months in which he had been absent from New York.

Still, the thought of suicide did not improve on acquaintance. While there was life there was hope. Why shouldn't he go back to New York, brave everything, and start anew to the best of his ability? Other men had pocketed their pride ; and, although his own pride was frightfully large to be submitted to such treatment, he did not know that the operation would give him any more discomfort than he was already enduring.

The thought resolved itself into decision when one day he chanced to meet in Boston a New Yorker with whom he had a casual acquaintance. After a little chat the man, who had been away from the city for months, remarked,—

"You're not married yet?"

"No," said Marge, with a grim smile.

"I thought I had heard that you were engaged to Miss Tramlay; and I wanted to congratulate you. An iron-house traveller whom I met a short time ago told me that Tramlay was getting rich very fast."

"I supposed," said Marge, with a dawn of interest, "that Miss Tramlay was to marry young Hayn."

"What! that country clerk of her father's?" said the man, with the confidence born of ignorance. "Nonsense! why, it seems only the other day that I heard some one laughing about that fellow's infatuation. Oh, no; now that they're rich, they'll want to marry their daughter to some one of social standing: indeed, I heard some one say as much. The mother is very ambitious in that line, you know."

Marge soon excused himself, lit a strong cigar, and betook himself to a solitary walk and some hard thinking. There was perhaps a grand point to be made on that fellow's suggestion. From what he knew of Mrs. Tramlay,—and he informed himself that no one knew that lady better,—he would not be surprised if an approved society man might now be entirely welcome as a husband for Lucia, even if he were as poor as a church mouse. And Lucia herself—had she not always longed for larger and more prominent society than she had yet enjoyed?

Before his cigar was burned out, Marge had bought a ticket for New York, determined to make a bold stroke for fortune where he felt that he had at heart

one faithful friend to aid him.   His imagination and
pride combined to cheer him on ; he would reappear
at Tramlay's, see how the land lay, and if the signs
were encouraging he would propose at once, first
taking Mrs. Tramlay into his confidence.   He had
lost enough by hesitation ; now he would adopt entirely new tactics, and there was no pleasanter way
to begin than by proposing to Lucia.   As he had told
himself before, she was a very pretty girl, and fully
competent, with such guidance as he would give her,
to make the most of her new advantages.

Reaching New York at nightfall, he lost no time
in dressing with extreme care and making his way
to the Tramlay abode.   He would have no difficulty
in explaining his long absence to the ladies ; perhaps
they had heard of his disaster in E. & W., but he
could tell them that he had been largely interested
in a rich silver-mine ever since.   There would be
nothing untrue in that statement ; had he not been
so deeply interested that he could not sleep a wink
during the week while the title to the Brighthope
mine—curse the rocky hole !—was first in doubt?
Besides, women were sure to talk, and equally sure
not to diminish the size of a story while telling it :
quite likely his tale, repeated by Mrs. Tramlay and
Lucia, might have the effect of restoring him to the
regard of the many people who estimate a man solely
by his money.

As he entered the house he was satisfied that his
operations would not be postponed by the announcement "not at home," for through the open door he
heard familiar voices in the rear of the parlor, and he

saw several heads bent over a table. None of them seemed to belong to strangers: so he entered with the freedom to which long acquaintance entitled him. The backs of the entire party were towards him, so his presence was not observed: besides, an animated discussion seemed to be going on between Lucia and Margie.

"I think you're real mean," he heard Margie say. Then he heard Lucia reply,—

"No, I'm not. Am I, mamma?"

"No," said Mrs. Tramlay, as Marge approached close enough to see that they were looking at the floor-plan of a house, spread upon the table.

"My heart is set upon having that room for my very own," said Margie. "The young lady of the family always has first choice, after her parents."

"Not where there is a bride to be provided for," Mrs. Tramlay replied.

"Well said, mamma. There, Margie," said Lucia; "that room is for Phil and me."

"Here," said Tramlay, entering from the library, with a large sheet of paper in his hand, "is the plan of—— Why, Marge!—bless my soul!—when did you get back, old fellow?"

"Mr. Marge!" exclaimed the three ladies in chorus, as they hastily arose.

"What! only just come in?" asked Tramlay. "And of course there was such a clatter here, there being three women together, that nobody could hear a word."

Apparently the ladies did not agree with the head of the family, for Mrs. Tramlay looked at the visitor pityingly and Lucia dropped her eyes and blushed. But Margie was equal to the situation : her eyes danced as she exclaimed,—

"Just in time to see the plans of the villa we're to have at Haynton Bay. See? This is the principal chamber floor ; it fronts that way, toward the water, and I've just been cheated out of the darlingest room of all : it's been set apart as sacred to the bride and groom. As if the silly things would care to look at water or anything else but each other !"

"It will be as handsome a house as there is on the coast," said Tramlay, "though your humble servant will be its owner. Say, old fellow, you need New York air : you don't look as well as usual."

"A long day of travel,—that is all," said Marge, with a feeble smile that seemed reluctant to respond to the demand imposed upon it.

Mrs. Tramlay rang for a servant, and whispered,—

"A glass of wine for Mr. Marge."

"Haynton Bay is booming," remarked Tramlay. "Have you heard any particulars recently?"

"None at all," drawled Marge : "I have been so busy that—— Thank you, Mrs. Tramlay," he said, with a nod and a glance, as the wine appeared.

"We're doing capitally," said Tramlay. "It begins to look as if, in spite of all the extra land on which old Hayn bought us options, there won't be enough sites to meet the demand."

The news and the wine—both were needed—raised Marge's spirits so that he ceased to fear he would faint. He finally collected wits and strength enough to say,—

"It's just the time for me to sell out, then?"

"Sell out?" echoed Tramlay. "It's just the time to hold on to it. I don't know of anything, anywhere, that's making a respectable fraction of the profit that there is in our little company, when the smallness of the investment is considered. I believe, too, we could make twice as much if there was some one who knew buyers well enough to charge appropriate prices. We've been selling at set figures, regardless of what some people might be persuaded to pay; prices of such property may as well be fancy, you know, for those who want it will have it at any price. But we've nobody to give proper attention to it: Phil's time is so fully occupied——"

"On account of——" interpolated Margie, pinching her sister's arm.

"Margie!" said Mrs. Tramlay, severely.

"He is so very busy——" resumed Tramlay.

"Being papa's partner," said Margie. "Have you seen the new sign 'Tramlay and Hayn' yet? Lu goes down town every day in our carriage, and I don't believe it's for anything but to look at that sign—— Oh, mamma, you hurt me cruelly then."

"Well," said Tramlay, "if I may be permitted to finish a sentence, I'd like to say that if you've an hour or two a day of spare time on your hands you could do a first-rate thing for the company, as well as yourself, by keeping an eye on this property. There's so much in it that I've had half a mind to devote myself to it and leave Phil to attend to iron; there's——"

"For Phil can do it," said Margie. "You must

have heard of his great Lake and Gulfside order: everybody said it was the greatest——"

" Margie," said Mrs. Tramlay, in ill-disguised anger, "go to your room, at once. Your father shall be allowed to talk without interruption."

"Thank you, my dear," said Tramlay. "As I was saying, Marge, there's no easier way to make that property bring twice as much money than for you, with your knowledge of who is who in New York, to give some personal attention to it."

"Thanks for the suggestion," said Marge. "I'll think about it. At present, however, I think I'll say good-by and seek some rest. I merely dropped in for a moment, to pay my respects."

" Lu," shouted Margie from the head of the stairs, as Marge was donning his light overcoat in the hall, "don't let Mr. Marge go until you show him that cunning little lovers'-nook on the plan of the house-front."

Mrs. Tramlay hurried to the hall and pressed Marge's hand : he looked down an instant, whispered, "Thank you," and departed.

CHAPTER XXVIII.

"AND E'EN THE FATES WERE SMILING."

"WELL, Lou Ann," said farmer Hayn one morning when the month of May had reached that stage when farmers forget their coats except on Sundays, "it'll seem 'most like takin' boarders again to have such a big crowd of city folks in the house, won't it?"

"Not quite as bad as that," said Mrs. Hayn, carefully moving an iron over one of the caps which she reserved for grand occasions. "Only Mr. and Mrs. Tramlay an' the two gals."

"Well, you ortn't to forget that Phil is city folks now, an—— I declare to gracious, I believe I forgot to tell you that Miss Dinon,—that splendid gal I told you about, that owns a lot of stock in the company, —Phil's writ that like enough she'll come down too. She an' her mother want to pick a lot for a house for themselves before it's too late for much of a choice."

"Well, I can't understand it yet," said Mrs. Hayn, carefully picking the lace edging of the cap into the proper *négligé* effect. "It seems like a dream. Here's me, that's sometimes been almost a-dyin' to get away from this farm an' into the city, an' there's a whole passel of city folks goin' to leave their palaces in New York an' come down here to live on little pieces of our farm an' other farms along the ridge. I tell you, I can't understand it."

"Well," said the farmer, picking some bits of oat chaff from his shirt-sleeve, "it ain't always easy to understand city folks at first sight. Now, there's that feller Marge. When I fust saw him in New York I wouldn't have give him his salt for any work he'd do in the country. Yet now look at him! Them roads an' drives through the company's property wouldn't have been half so near done if he hadn't come down here an' took hold to hurry things along for the spring trade. Why, some of them fellers that's doin' the work has worked for me on the farm, off an' on, for years, an' I thought I knowed how to get as much out of 'em as ther' was in 'em; but, bless your soul, he manages 'em a good deal better."

"They do say he's a master-hand at managin'," Mrs. Hayn admitted, "an' that it's partly because he takes right hold himself, instead of standin' round bossin', like most city men."

"Takes hold? Why, he works as if he'd been brought up at it, which I'm certain sure he never was. You can't see the fun of it, because you never saw him in New York. Why, if you could have seen him there you'd have thought that a gate-post with two pegs in the bottom of it would have had as much go as him. I've reelly took a likin' to him. More'n once I've let him know that I wouldn't mind if he'd leave the hotel in the village an' put up with us, but somehow he didn't seem to take to it."

"That's strange, ain't it?" said Mrs. Hayn, with a quizzical look that made her husband stare.

"Oh !" said the old man, after a little reflection.

"You're growin' dretful old an' short-sighted, Reuben," said Mrs. Hayn; and the farmer made haste to change the subject of conversation.

A day or two later the party from the city arrived, and great was the excitement in the village. Sol Mantring's wife, who had learned of what was expected, made a trip to Hayn Farm daily on one pretext or other, reaching there always just before the time of the arrival of the train from the city, received the deserved reward of her industry, and before sunset of the day on which the party arrived everybody in the village knew that when Lucia stepped from the carriage, at the farm-house door, Mrs. Hayn caught her in her arms and almost hugged the life out of her. Everybody knew, also, that the party was to be there for only twenty-four hours.

"The shortness of the time at their disposal was probably the reason that Phil and Lucia disappeared almost immediately after the meal which quickly followed their arrival. They went to the lily-pond ; there were no lilies yet upon the water, but the couple did not notice their absence ; they could see them just where they should be,—just where they were, ten months before. They got again into the old birch-bark canoe ; it was not as clean as it should have been for the sake of Lucia's expensive travelling-dress, for the small boys of the Hayn family had not taken as good care of it as Phil would do, but Phil made a cushion of leaves, which Lucia slowly expanded into a couch, as she half reclined while she identified the scenes which her farmer-boy guide and boatman had shown her the summer before. Phil thought her expression angelic as she dreamily gazed about her ; yet when her eyes reverted to him, as they frequently did, he informed himself that there were even gradations of angelic expression.

They even rode in the old beach-wagon ; the ocean was still as cold as winter ; bathing was out of the question ; but Phil had a persistent fancy for re- minding his sweetheart of every change there had been in their relations, and in himself; and Lucia understood him.

"It's dreadfully mean of those two to go off by themselves, and not help us have any fun," com- plained Margie to Agnes Dinon, when the latter returned from a stroll with Mr. and Mrs. Tramlay, during which she had selected a satisfactory cottage- site. "Let's have a run. I know every foot of this country. Do you see that clump of dwarfed cedars off yonder on the ridge, with the sky for a background ? They're lovely : I've tried again and again to sketch them. Come over and look at them."

Away the couple plodded. As they approached the clump they saw that a road had been partly sunk in front of it ; and as they drew nearer they saw a man sodding a terrace which sloped from the ridge to the road.

"That's not right," said another man, who was looking on. "That sod must be laid more securely, or the first rain will wash it away. I'll show you how to do it. See here."

"Agnes Dinon !" exclaimed Margie, in a tone which suggested that a mouse, or at least a snake, was in close proximity. "Do you hear that voice?—do you see that man? Do you know who he is? That is the elegant Mr. Marge."

Miss Dinon manifested surprise, but she quickly whispered,—

"Sh-h-h! Yes, I knew he was here, looking after the company's interests. He is one of the directors, you know."

"Yes, I know; but see his hat and his clothes,—and his brown hands. This is simply killing! Oh, if I had crayons and paper, or, better still, a camera! The girls at home won't believe me when I tell them: they'll think it too utterly preposterous."

"Why should you tell them?" asked Agnes, turning away. "Isn't it entirely honorable for a man to be caring for his own and fulfilling his trust, especially when so valuable a property as this is demands his attention?"

"Yes, yes, you dear old thing; but——" .

"'Sh-h!'" whispered Agnes, for just then Marge climbed the slope and appeared a little way in front of them, shouting back at the man,—

"Cut your next sod here: this seems to have thicker grass."

Suddenly he saw the ladies and recognized them. It was too late to run, as he assuredly would have done if warned in time, but he had the presence of mind to shout to his workman,—

"No, it isn't, either. Get the next from the old place!"

"Good-morning, Mr. Marge," said Miss Dinon, with a frank smile and an outstretched hand.

22

Marge raised his hat, bowed, and replied,—

"The hand of the laboring-man is sometimes best shaken in spirit. I assure you, though, I appreciate the compliment."

"Then don't deny me the honor," said Miss Dinon. "It's a positive pleasure to see a man doing something manly. It is my misfortune that I see men only in the city, you know, and doing nothing."

Her hand was still extended, so Marge took it, again raising his hat. Margie turned away; the situation was so comical to her that she felt she must laugh, and she knew by experience that her laughter was sometimes uncontrollable when fairly started.

"Mr. Tramlay says you've worked wonders since you've been here," said Miss Dinon, as Marge released her hand; "and, as old Mr. Hayn is his authority, I have no doubt it is so."

"I imagine that I deserve the company's thanks," Marge replied, "though I'm astonished at having mastered some portions of the work so quickly. I think I can astonish you, also, by an honest confession : I really wish something of this sort had turned up years ago; I'm a great deal happier at it than I ever was while worrying my wits over stocks in Wall Street. I think the work far more honorable and manly, too. You're quite at liberty to repeat this to any of our mutual friends in the city : I'm sure 'twill amuse them, and their laughter won't annoy me a particle."

"They wouldn't laugh," said Miss Dinon, "if they could breathe this glorious air awhile, and foresee the

c

gold which this ground will yield, unless appearances are deceitful."

The old beach-wagon, a quarter of a mile away, crawled up the grassy slope from the long stretch of sand, and Phil stopped, as of old, to let the horse breathe after his hard tug at the deep-sinking wheels.

"What a picture those two people make on the hill yonder, beside that green clump!" said Lucia. "Why, the woman is Agnes,—there is Margie, picking daisies far to the right,—and the man Agnes is talking to is some common workman. What a splendid woman she is! She can be as independent as she likes, and no one ever mistakes her meaning. Imagine any other girl of our set standing on a country hill-side, chatting with some boor!"

"Boor?" echoed Phil, running a whole gamut of intonations. "Do you know who that boor is? I recognized him at sight: he was in the village as we passed through, but it didn't seem kind to call attention to him."

"Who is he? Do tell me."

"Mr. Marge."

"Philip Hayn!" exclaimed Lucia. "Do turn the wagon away, so we don't seem to be looking at them."

"Consistency, thy name is not woman," said Phil, after complying with the request, for Lucia was kneeling on the back seat of the wagon and peering through the little window in the dingy old curtain.

"Not to revive any unpleasant memories," said Marge, after he and Miss Dinon had chatted several moments, as co-investors, about the property, "but merely to call attention to the irony of fate, it seems

odd to me to contrast to-day and a certain day several
years ago. Laugh about it, I beg of you, because I
call attention to it only for its laughable side. To-day
you do me the honor—which I never shall forget—of
pressing your hand upon me, although no stranger
could distinguish me from one of my workmen.
Then, when in a different sense I wanted your hand,
and had the temerity to think myself worthy of it,
you withheld it."

Miss Dinon did not laugh; she looked off toward
the sea, and said,—

"You were not then as you are to-day."

"Thank you. But if I had been?"

Again Miss Dinon looked toward the sea, and
said,—

"I might perhaps have been more appreciative."

"And to-day," said Marge, gently taking the lady's
finger-tips,—"no, not to-day, but hereafter, is it impossible that I should honestly earn·it?"

"Who knows," said Agnes, gently, "but you?"

"Phil!" gasped Lucia, from the back of the old
beach-wagon, "he is kissing her hand!"

"Umph!" said Phil: "what can that mean?"

Lucia looked at him soberly, and replied,—

"What a question for you, of all men, to ask!"

"Why, 'tis only an old-fashioned form of salutation
or adieu," said Phil, "I have your own word for it:
don't you remember?"

For answer, Lucia's eyes looked from beneath their
lashes so provokingly that Phil stepped across his
seat and hid each under his moustache for a second
or two.

CHAPTER XXIX.

SO THEY WERE MARRIED.

As Mrs. Tramlay remarked at an earlier stage of this narrative, June was as late in the season as was fashionable for a wedding. Thanks, however, to a large infusion of the unexpected into the plans of all concerned, Lucia's wedding did not have to be deferred until after June. All the invited guests pronounced it as pretty an affair of its kind as the season had known, and the more so because the bride and groom really made a very handsome and noteworthy couple,—an occurrence quite as unusual in the city as in the country.

The only complaints that any one heard were from Haynton and vicinity. The friends and acquaintances of the Hayn family held many informal meetings and voted it an outrage that when such a lot of money was to be spent on a wedding it should all be squandered on New York people, who had so much of similar blessings that they did not know how to appreciate them, instead of Haynton, where the couple would sooner or later make their home; for had not Phil selected a villa-site for himself, on his father's old farm?

No invitations by card reached Haynton, but Phil's

pastor went down quietly to the city to assist at the
marriage-service, by special arrangement, and Hayn
Farm of course sent a large delegation, and the head
of the family saw to it that none of the masculine
members wore garments of the Sarah Tweege cut
longer than was required to make a thorough change
at a reputable clothing-store. As for Mrs. Hayn, her
prospective daughter found time enough to assume
filial duties in advance, and the old lady was so
pleased with the change that ever afterward she was
what the late lamented Mr. Boffin would have
termed "a high-flyer at fashion."

But there are souls who laugh to scorn any such
trifling obstructions as lack of formal invitation, and
one of these was Sol Mantring's wife. She tormented
her husband until that skipper found something that
would enable him to pay the expense of running his
sloop to New York and back; his wife sailed with
him as sole passenger, and on the morning of the
wedding she presented herself at the church an
hour before the appointed time, and in raiment such
as had not been seen in that portion of New York
since the days when sullen brownstone fronts began
to disfigure farms that had been picturesque and
smiling. She laid siege to the sexton; she told him
who she was, and how she had held Phil in her arms
again and again when he had the whooping-cough,
and yet again when he had scarlet fever, although she
ran the risk of taking the dread malady home to her
own children, and the sexton, in self-defence, was
finally obliged to give her a seat in the gallery, over the
rail of which, as near the altar as possible, her elabo-

rately-trimmed Sunday bonnet caught the eyes of
every one who entered. What all Haynton did not
know about that wedding, three days later, was not
worth knowing ; it was a thousand times more satisfactory than the combined reports in the morning
papers, all of which Mrs. Mantring carried home with
her and preserved between the leaves of her family
Bible for the remainder of her days, and every one
in the village read them, even Sarah Tweege, who
magnanimously waived the apparent slight implied
by Phil not having his wedding-suit made by her.

Mrs. Hayn, Senior, no longer had to wish in vain
for a place in the city where she might sometimes
forget the cares and humdrum of farm-house life.
Risky as the experiment seemed from the society
point of view, Lucia, backed by Margie, insisted
upon making her at home in the city whenever she
chose to come; and, although some friends of the
family would sometimes laugh in private over the
old lady's peculiarities of accent and grammar, there
were others who found real pleasure in the shrewd
sense and great heart that had been developed by a
life in which the wife had been obliged to be the
partner and equal of her husband.

Before a year passed there was another wedding.
Agnes Dinon changed her name without any mis-
givings; she had previously confessed to Lucia, who
in spite of the difference in years seemed to become
her favorite confidante, that she had always admired
some things about Mr. Marge, and that the business-
misfortunes which had compelled him to become the
active manager of the Haynton Bay Improvement

Company seemed to supply what had been lacking in his character and manner.

Other people who were no longer young were gainers by the culmination of the incidents narrated in this tale. Tramlay and his wife seemed to renew their youth under the influence of the new love that pervaded their home, and almost daily the merchant blessed his partner for gains more precious than those of business. He never wearied of rallying his wife on her early apprehensions regarding the acquaintance between her daughter and the young man from the country. Mrs. Tramlay's invariable reply was the question,—

"But who could have foreseen it? I can't, to this day, understand how it all came about."

"Nor I," her husband would reply. "As I've said before, it's country luck. Nine men of every ten who amount to anything in New York come from the country. Remember it, my dear, when next you have a daughter who you think needs a husband."

THE END.